W9-CES-725

NEW HANOVER COUNTY
PUBLIC LIBRARY

If found, please return to:
201 Chestnut St.
Wilmington, NC 28401
(910) 798-6300
http://www.nhclibrary.org

The Coloring Book

The Coloring Book

A COMEDIAN SOLVES
RACE RELATIONS IN AMERICA

Colin Quinn

GRAND CENTRAL
PUBLISHING

NEW YORK   BOSTON

NEW HANOVER COUNTY
PUBLIC LIBRARY
201 CHESTNUT STREET
WILMINGTON, NC 28401

Copyright © 2015 by CQE, Inc.
All rights reserved. In accordance with the U.S. Copyright Act of 1976, the scanning, uploading, and electronic sharing of any part of this book without the permission of the publisher constitute unlawful piracy and theft of the author's intellectual property. If you would like to use material from the book (other than for review purposes), prior written permission must be obtained by contacting the publisher at permissions@hbgusa.com. Thank you for your support of the author's rights.

Grand Central Publishing
Hachette Book Group
1290 Avenue of the Americas
New York, NY 10104

HachetteBookGroup.com

Printed in the United States of America

RRD-C

First Edition: June 2015
10 9 8 7 6 5 4 3 2 1

Grand Central Publishing is a division of Hachette Book Group, Inc. The Grand Central Publishing name and logo is a trademark of Hachette Book Group, Inc.

The Hachette Speakers Bureau provides a wide range of authors for speaking events. To find out more, go to www.hachettespeakersbureau.com or call (866) 376-6591.

The publisher is not responsible for websites (or their content) that are not owned by the publisher.

Library of Congress Cataloging-in-Publication Data
Quinn, Colin.
   The coloring book : a comedian solves race relations in America / Colin Quinn.
      pages cm
   ISBN 978-1-4555-0759-7 (hardback) — ISBN 978-1-4789-0379-6 (audiobook) — ISBN 978-1-4789-0380-2 (audio download)
   1. United States—Race relations—Humor.   I. Title.
   PN6231.R25Q85 2015
   818'.602—dc23
                                                          2014049903

This is dedicated to all the mixed-race, polyglot, mestizo, multiracial, biracial, triracial people out there. May there someday be wars based only on personality differences.

Contents

The Coloring
Book

Park Slope Rainbow

TODAY IT MAY LOOK LIKE A SWISS VILLAGE, BUT PARK SLOPE, Brooklyn, in the 1970s was maybe the most mixed—integrated, they called it—neighborhood in the history of the world. Park Slope in the seventies was magical. It was a special place to grow up. Everyone felt it, except the murder victims.

I would walk home from Intermediate School 88, past Puerto Rican blocks, black blocks, Italian blocks, Irish blocks, the Arab deli, the Chinese takeout place, the first Dominican bodega, and the remnants of what was once a big Polish neighborhood.

One block would look as bombed-out as the South Bronx and the next would look as clean and affluent as...

Park Slope today. My block was Puerto Rican on one corner, black on the other, and Irish, Italian, and Jewish in the middle. From kindergarten through high school, we had every kind of kid in my house all the time. So I should be the only person in the country allowed to talk about race.

And yet what I've seen more and more in the past thirty years are well-meaning people who rolled out of some annoying suburb and then moved to New York and immediately began trying to regulate everyone's language and thoughts. People are so very afraid of offending that they act like diversity doesn't even exist. As a result, there is this weird impulse in American culture today to say, "We're all exactly the same." To celebrate diversity as long as you don't point out anyone's differences.

If you ask people to describe somebody, they'll avoid saying their color. If pushed, their voice drops with shame and regret that they still think in those terms. You even hear cops going, even in the police blotter: "The suspect was 5'10" and 280 pounds—and that's not fat-shaming, we're just pointing it out."

I'm tired of humorless activist people decreeing that we only use these words and never those, and that we "check our privilege," in case we say the wrong thing and "trigger" someone. Supposedly nonjudgmental judgmentalism used to be what Southern California was for, but now it's encroaching even here in New York—where people are supposed to come *to* judge things. It's not the place to re-create the boring suburban landscape of your childhoods.

I don't like being bossed around—and that's not using the word "bossy" in a gender-specific manner—especially when it comes to humor, and especially not by the least funny people on earth. Across the country, the sexist office asshole has been replaced by the flat-affect, dead-eyed modern-day Puritan. Both groups—the old-school assholes and the neo-Puritans—share a common goal: to wipe the smile off of everyone's face.

People who condemn other people for talking about race are usually members of what my friend Harry calls the "never-been-punched-in-the-face club"—smug, obnoxious people who feel very confident in their ability to say anything they want about what other people should and shouldn't do because they've never received a nice shot in the grill.

New Yorkers used to be straight shooters and loud-mouths. They spoke their mind. The opinionated cabbie. The construction worker. The counterperson. The merchant. The old man at the bar. The guy selling pretzels. You can buy a better pretzel anywhere in the country, but what made the New York pretzel the best was the shitty, sarcastic attitude of the guy selling it. When I was growing up, tourists didn't come here for the Rockefeller Tree or "nice place to bring your kids." They came to be told to fuck off by a real New Yorker.

Native New Yorkers have always had the abrupt, honest tone we need when talking about race. It's so much better than today's lethally fake one: "I'm sorry you feel that way."

"That's very interesting. I never thought about it like that."
"I'm not sure I'm comfortable with that terminology." A
strained smile of acceptance and a golf clap.

So all the nuances go unexplored. There are degrees of
racism. Yes, unlike a little bit pregnant, you can be a little
bit racist! There's a difference between a white supremacist
and a little old white lady who slightly clutches her purse
when a black guy gets in the elevator with her; between a
white guy who doesn't hire black people and a white guy
who flinches the tiniest bit when he sees a photo of his teenage daughter with her new "friend" at a Kendrick Lamar
concert.

This is not an ethnic joke book: drunk Irish black guys
with big dicks, bad Asian drivers. I don't want to deal with
them because to do so would be to beat a dead horse, and
I don't want to offend animal rights activists.

Different cultures are different. If you go to Queens, you
can see restaurant signs with pictures of exotic fish with
human faces, flamingos fighting over a burrito on Roosevelt
Avenue, roasted guinea pigs hanging on a clothesline in Elm-
hurst, a mongoose spitting from a fire escape. That's what I
want to talk about.

These days, the supposedly enlightened response to most
questions is, "Who's to say?" My answer: *Everyone's* to say.
That used to be New York's motto.

TRIGGER WARNING: *This book may be harmful to
impressionable adults. It may raise distressing, troubling,*

problematic concerns. It may be "tone-deaf" in today's climate. Given the fact that it's coming from a place of white Eurocentric unconscious paternalistic fear of "the other," it may add to divisiveness. It may contain stereotypes or generalizing. If offended, please alert Twitter or your favorite local blogger.

I

Dashiki Red, Black & Green

NOTHING MAKES A ROOM TENSE UP FASTER THAN TALKING about black people when you're white. People will make jokes about Europeans all day long: *Germans are Nazis. Everyone hates the French.* But as soon as you start talking about people who aren't white and you are white, everyone gets anxious. Is this what we're striving for, avoidance of the topic at all costs? Frozen smiles and polite, strained looks?

To me, there are two routes to take when it comes to dealing with race: Stay separate and pretend we aren't different at all, or live together and acknowledge the ways in which race sometimes does actually matter. Of course, the compromise of living halfway together and pretending we are all the same is working out wonderfully.

* * *

Black people showed up in New York City in the early 1920s, in the white Manhattan suburb called Harlem. Before that, black people lived only down South. Until 1963, everyone wanted to be white. Wingtips, and whistling big band music on your way to the foundry, slaughterhouse, or brewery; you walked white, tipped your unironic fedora to the ladies, and shook hands with a hearty "How do'ya do?" Everyone acted white—even Malcom X straightened his hair. There was a dress code: No jeans. No sneakers for anyone over twelve. You had to wear a shirt and tie if you were a guy. Even on construction sites: shirt and tie. Health food was a can of mixed fruit with syrup and food coloring.

Then one day in May of 1964, two soul brothers (as they were known back then) ran into each other on the street. Instead of the usual "Hiya, pal, how's tricks?" and a firm grasp of each other's hands, one guy put out his palm and said "Gimme some skin, Jack" and the other guy slapped his palm and that was that. They changed the greeting! That's kind of a major thing if you think about it. People are greeting each other all over the country, maybe one out of every three people every day. That's 191.9 million people in the U.S. back then. That's about sixty-four million greetings a day. And black people changed probably half of those. Black culture then ruled New York City. Before, there had been watch repair, TV repair, shoe repair, and clothing repair, even though everybody owned a sewing machine. Suddenly, even my father was wearing a hip, open shirt and growing a beard. People were smoking joints, the Knicks were the stars of New York, and people listened to Gamble and Huff music while wearing giant shoes.

* * *

I moved to Park Slope when I was seven. Before that I was in Bay Ridge, then Flatbush, but Park Slope was crazy. Wild white kids, wild Puerto Ricans, but nobody was wilder than the black kids. When us white kids or Puerto Rican kids would steal candy or jump on the back of buses, we were still scared to get caught and have our mothers find out. But the black kids were not scared of any store owner or bus driver. They'd start yelling back at adults. "Get off me! Tell my mother!" and the store owners wouldn't tell, because they knew if they did, sure, they *could* get a sympathetic woman who thanked them and shook her head and said "I don't know what to do with him," BUT they *might* get the Ghetto Avenger mother who came running in with a string of curses, knocking over the display case and threatening the owner for putting his hands on her kid.

Our store owners were all characters. They all had growths or warts or scars and Coke-bottle glasses. They were usually either morbidly obese or tubercular. They were prejudiced but not racist.

Danny, the Jewish candy store owner: "Hey, you kid, don't jump the line. The colored lady was next. You respect your elders. Now you go to the back. It's the colored lady, the Spanish girl and the Chinaman, and then you. You learn how to behave!"

He was a nice guy and if you asked him what race he hated the most, I bet he would say Germans first, because he was a Jew that grew up in the thirties. People can be prejudiced against groups based on their experience (not just ignorance), but that doesn't mean they don't like the individuals. Most black people hate "white people" as a concept but they like a lot...well, some...okay a few, white people.

* * *

My first day at I.S. 88, I was walking down the hall and a group of black kids were coming from the other direction chanting, "Ungawa, Black Power. Destroy, white boy." I thought, *I hope that's not the school song.* Often during fights, the black kids would chant, "Fight, fight, nigger and a white! The white turned red, and the nigger dropped dead!"

A lot of white kids in the old neighborhood would use the word "nigger," and that didn't make them racist. They even sometimes used the word in anger—even in anger toward a black person they knew—and that didn't make them racist either.

Ohhhh, you heard me. Using that word wasn't the entirety of people's feelings toward or relationship to the black race. Someone might have an unpleasant interaction with a black person and use the word, and yet at the same time have tons of close black friends who they would die for. Those black friends might hate "white people," but they would have white friends who they would die for, too.

These are contradictions, but most of life is contradictory. There are no absolutes, unless you're an idiot with a naïve belief that life is only one way, always and forever. When you're just theorizing about it, absolutes make sense, but when you're living a real life and having actual hot-and-cold relationships with real people, shit gets complicated.

* * *

"Yo, shut up, you black parakeet!"

"Who you calling a parakeet, you black bitch?"

"Who you calling bitch, bitch? My brother gonna come up to this school and bust your ass."

"Shut up, your head look like a snail shell."

"So what, you got slave hair!"

"You got old-lady ears."

"Shut up, you live in back of the hardware store, come to school smelling like cut keys!"

They were funny those kids. They'd come rolling into class like they just bought the place, making fun of each other's financial status—who's on welfare, food stamps, AFDC, SSI: They knew the system backward and forward. They'd sing songs about each other's mothers on the 67 bus home. "Me and Mrs., Mrs. Richardson" to the tune of "Me and Mrs. Jones." Or the song "I'll Always Love My Mama" was almost asking for it. Some kid would look sincerely at another and sing, "I'll always love your mama, she's my favorite girl." And "It's a sha-a-a-ame...the way I mess around with your mom."

They were never boring. One time, the teacher was yelling, it was really tense, and this kid Ralph opened the door and looked directly at a kid named Trent like he was delivering the most important message in the world. He said, "Trent, your father wanted me to tell you to leave the shoes on the back steps of the school—he's got to go to work." Then he closed the door and left us all there for that stunned pause until everyone, even the teacher who'd been furious with us, couldn't help laughing.

Since I was little, black people have been at war with the system. Most people came into I.S. 88 with varying degrees of resigned acceptance. The Jews and Asians were listening to the teacher. The Italians were killing time till the union job. The Puerto Ricans were using it as a singles mixer. The black girls came in with Sugar Babies, Fruit Stripe gum, and Pixy Stix. They'd walk around the class, figuring out where to sit. "Who sittin' here? Can you change seats so I could sit next to my friend?" The teacher would say, "Josephine, sit down." Josephine would arch her back and announce to the room in outrage, "Lincoln freed the slaves!" then sit down and start eating squares off her candy necklace.

Five minutes later the black guys would float in. Somewhere between a John Wayne swagger and a Renaissance prince, they'd enter like Medici popes coming by to check up on Michelangelo. They'd put a number 2 pencil in their Afro as a way of acknowledging they were in a classroom.

They'd sit splay-legged halfway out in the aisle, digging the scene with a gangster lean (as the song went). If a black kid gave an answer to a question, it was fine, but only if it was a laconic throwaway. Like he was so cool the answer just slid out. He would take the toothpick out of his mouth..."The, um...Magna Carta"—and then immediately back to the toothpick. You could get away with it if you had the style, but if there was any lapdog or enthusiasm or wish for the teacher's approval showing, there would be a loud *tsssss*, like letting the air out of a basketball.

* * *

Fights were always happening. It seemed like there was a fight every day. Either somebody was threatening to fight you, or you were hearing that your friend was getting into a fight, or your little brother was fighting, or there was a fight happening right now and you'd better hurry if you were gonna catch the end of it. Then people would say "I heard so-and-so had a fight," and you could say "Yeah, I saw it."

I remember having to fight. Some kid was next to me in line and said, "You wanna fight?" and I couldn't say, "Well, that's coming out of left field." I had to gulp and say "Okay!" The next thing I know, I'm rolling around in the hallway with a bunch of kids cheering like they're watching pay-per-view.

My first or second day of class in Park Slope, I'm walking in the halls and this little black kid came by and blocked my path and said, "Hey, white boy, gimme a quarter." I said no, laughed, and pushed him. Suddenly, I heard, "You push my cousin, you freckle-faced strawberry?" (As a child I had a lovely face full of freckles, like a young Julianne Moore.) It was the old bait and switch! This big kid was there. Then he pushed me. The security guard broke it up, and the kid said to me, "I'll see you at three o'clock."

So we go back to class and now I know I'm fighting at three o'clock. All the kids in class are excited, because everyone loves to see a fight. And my stomach hurt because this kid looks like a real fighter. He had a mini Afro, which was usually a bad sign. A big Afro meant a fun playboy. But a mini Afro parted on the side was only for the hardest of hard rocks.

As all boys know, there's no experience like waiting until three o'clock for a fight with a kid that you know is probably going to beat you severely. A teacher is bullshitting on about long division and I'm just trying to figure out if there's a way I can maneuver this fight to the curb, so I can get a passing truck to do my dirty work for me.

People now say you're supposed to report bullying. In those days the teachers were trying to survive for themselves. They were trying to hurry home, get on the train before it got dark. I saw a teacher get beat up by a parent in grammar school. The parent stormed into the classroom and beat his own kid around the room, then turned and punched the teacher in the chest when he tried to intervene. Then the parent stared at the class silently, like, "Anyone have a problem with what just happened?" And we all sat there quietly, hoping we weren't next.

One time, this kid Jasper's mom was coming up to school with her brother or boyfriend, definitely there to complain about how the school was treating Jasper. A kid was looking out the window. "Oh shit," he said, "here comes Jasper's mom." We all ran over to the window and when we turned around, the door was open and the teacher was gone.

My uncle Eddie was a teacher at Franklin K. Lane. The students lit one of his coworkers on fire. So when the teachers would see a fight they'd pretend it wasn't happening. For half a shithead like me, they would say, "Aren't you the kid that makes jokes about my sideburns in the back of the room? Good luck, big mouth."

But back to that day: All the kids are crowded around like Roman soldiers at the Crucifixion, and they're all chanting like little demons. I'm surprised some kid wasn't selling programs and pretzels. This kid and I begin to fight, and I can tell almost immediately that any chance I have is going to come from wrestling, because this kid is just a little too advanced with the way he's holding his hands. I grab him and he flips me into a group of kids and jumps on me.

In those days, people really believed in the concept of a fair fight, and there were no group stompings. You had to fight it out man-to-man. If somebody tried to jump in, the whole world would beat their ass for trying to upset the forces of nature and society. But you would get in a fight after school and it was a big event. People love to see violence. And they loved you for being in the fight. Now kids just jump in and stomp kids half to death while chanting "Worldstar." In those days there was no YouTube, so after a few months of telling the story, you kept slightly changing it until you eventually won the fight.

The worst part of getting your ass kicked after school is retrieving your books and pencils that got scattered all over the place—all your little papers with stupid numbers from math on them that seemed meaningless now—and taking the Charlie Brown walk home.

But the thing about a fight is, even if you lose you're still a little bit of a celebrity for a few days. I didn't like that I got my ass kicked and that everybody watched me get my ass kicked, but I did like that I was not anonymous. It was similar to bombing in comedy, really. When it first happens you think that nothing could be more humiliating. Everybody is looking at you; some are horrified and pitying, some sadists are enjoying it. But either way, even if it's just for one day, everybody respects you for trying. And you realize you didn't die from it.

In those days, you had to fight for your train pass. The school would give you a pass that would enable you to travel for free on public transportation for a year. And every other kid in school knew that. Why didn't they just make them out of gold and stick them around your neck? In 1970s New York, the subway was violent and crime-ridden. And so you had to get beat up to defend your right to keep the pass so that you could get mugged on the subway on the way home.

I won some fights, too, but even when I won I still lost. There was this skinny black kid named Walter who was messing with me one day. We fought in front of the school and I emerged victorious. I got the better of him, as people used to say. I gave no further thought to that fool until the next fall, when he came in after summer vacation and must've put on six inches in height and forty pounds of steel. There's nothing more intimidating than when you can see muscles under a dashiki. This kid had turned into a monster. And I had the physique of Avril Lavigne. The first time I saw him in the hallway at school I didn't recognize him. We passed each other, and at the last second my eyes widened like I had just seen a ghost. (I probably did—my own.) Every time after that, we just nodded professionally. I know he didn't want to kick my ass because it would bring up a lot of questions as to what happened originally, and that could shame him in his new identity as Black Caesar of I.S. 88. It was what they call a détente. He had power, I had information.

* * *

People say kids are spoiled now. Good. It was the parents who were spoiled back then. Now, parents have to spend all this money on their kids' uniforms, Xboxes, PlayStations. Our parents bought one shitty ball and made up these "street games" they supposedly played in the Depression era that were, coincidentally, free. The games always took place on the stoop (free) or the curb (free), and the lamppost with the exposed electrical wiring could be home base (free). The balls would get caught in dirty gutters filled with oven grease, stale cigars, and refrigerator coolant. We'd breathe in the sewage from the sewer grates for two hours. "Go outside and play! It's healthier."

It was never parents watching the games. You'd get the amateur sportswriter on the stoop. It was: "You got no arm" or "He's fast but he's gonna be a fat teenager, you can tell by his calves."

There were two kinds of street games: violent games and games that would turn violent. We'd play skellies with bottle caps. To make a skelly board or to make bases, you'd have to cut up the street with a knife. In Hot Peas and Butter, you'd hide a belt and then whoever found it would whip the other kids until they got to home base. I once played with just one big kid, and he ended up trying to hang me with the belt. His father came home and yelled at him to put his belt back on, which really wasn't the root cause of the problem. I should've said, "Sir, your son's a psychotic. It's not a wardrobe malfunction."

Then there was Knuckles. This was a game where you'd have a deck of cards and the other person would pick from the deck, and if they picked a black 10, for example, they'd get ten soft smacks on the knuckles. But if they picked a red 10 they'd get ten hard smacks. And I forget what would cause the penalty, but for something you would have to suffer a "sandwich," which involved putting your hand on the ground, with half the deck of cards on either side of your hand, and a kid would stomp on your hand.

* * *

My comedy career peaked at thirteen, when I was the class clown. I was part of a class clown interracial comedy team— me and Charlie J. He was as funny as I was, but when he moved to Virginia, we disbanded the act. I was considered funny because I'd come over and start busting people's balls, which in my neighborhood was the ticket to the big time. Black people don't like veiled comments or irony. Their idea of funny is to say something to your face.

When I snuck out of class, I would *sneak* out. But the black kids would get up and walk out like they were above it all. If a naïve teacher asked where they were going, they'd look at him with irritation, like, "You really want to play this game?" If they condescended to answer, it would be matter-of-fact: "The nurse." Or "My mother need me to go downtown to Tillary" (or Adams or Schermerhorn or Livingston—any of the Brooklyn streets where you'd find the offices of city bureaucracy).

And if some substitute teacher from the suburbs said, "But you can't leave!" the kid would chuckle sadly and walk out after looking around the room to the rest of us like, "Please explain the dynamics here."

I was loud and attention-seeking and lazy. Today they would diagnose me with Attention Deficit Disorder and

I'd be getting some nice meds, but in those days, instead of ADD they just diagnosed you as a loudmouth future asshole. When he saw me coming, a friend's father who hated me used to say, "Here he is: the ham." There are always those friends' fathers who hate you.

Big kids, on the other hand, were my mortal enemies. I still hate people two years older than me. They should have separate schools for each grade. It was always the left-back kids who caused the biggest problems in class. Yeah, that's a good idea: Tell this kid, "You are not good at school, so we are going to keep you for an extra year. And we're going to place you in a room with a bunch of younger, smaller kids to further shame you." Gee, I wonder where that psychological powder keg is going to focus his rage.

Some people say about kids who enjoy watching their peers get hurt, "Oh, kids can be so cruel." Really? You ever see the celebrities at a boxing match? These are the richest and most successful people in the world. They are role models. And they pay thousands of dollars to get a seat up front to watch bloodshed and brain damage. They could be spending that Saturday night at a cancer ward. People either say bullying is the worst thing ever or they try to put a positive spin on it—it builds character. I suppose if by "character" you mean that you cover your teeth when you laugh because people called you Snaggletooth or you have a twitch because kids made fun of your limp, then I guess it builds character. I guess you could argue that PTSD prepares you for the real world. Sure. But talk to the fat kid, the short kid, and the short, fat kid before you tell me that. I don't want to hear about how bullying is good for your character from someone hot. Adversity builds character? Yes, if by "character" you mean homelessness, depression, suicidal ideation, and school shootings.

I was guilty of it, too. I made fun of kids. I pushed around a couple. One time, I got beat up after I beat up a kid—because this other kid didn't like my unsportsmanlike conduct. I won the fight, and then I kneed the kid in his leg as I got up. So this other kid goes, "You didn't have to knee him," and *he* kicked my ass, and what do you think his last move was as I was lying there?

* * *

Park Slope's Seventh Avenue used to have its own fish market, meat market, candy store, luncheonette, bakery, and deli. All the luncheonettes, fish markets, and meat markets were Italian. Bakeries were German. Delis were Jewish. Bodegas were Spanish. If you were in a bodega and under the age of ten, they knew you were there to rob. From ten to fifteen, you were there to buy stuff that you weren't supposed to buy.

When I was growing up, there was no law. No "You must be eighteen to buy cigarettes."

When an adult said, "Son, you're too young to be smoking," you would respond, between puffs, "I got permission."

"These are for your mother, right?" the guy at the typical bodega might ask as you bought a pack.

"Uh, yeah," you would say, unconvincingly.

"You know, smoking is very bad. It's no good. Little boy, you should not smoke. That's for adults." But he'd still sell them to you. As long as you told him it was for your mother, that was legally binding. It would hold up in court.

To save time, you'd hope to get the guy's wife. She was always so mad at him about his girlfriend that she actually sort of wanted his business to go under, so she'd sell you whatever you wanted, coldly tossing it across the counter. You got that sort of personal touch everywhere you went in Brooklyn in those days.

In each store, regardless of ethnicity, everyone was rude. Shopkeepers all yelled, in various accents, "What do you want?" At the luncheonette, they would smoke cigars in the face of little kids eating grilled cheese sandwiches. The customers were rude, too: "Give me a liverwurst without too much mustard!" "Give me a half a pound of chuck chop!" "Go easy on the relish!" The customers came out of the womb dissatisfied, believing they were being cheated: "Ma, don't be stingy with the breast milk." That's how everybody ordered. At the pizza parlor it was "Gimme a slice," and you had the picky bastards who thought they were special—"Not from that pie, from the one under it." There was always a better pie that was being hidden from them.

The candy store on Garfield and Seventh was Jewish. The owner, Danny, the one who was prejudiced but not racist, had a tragic story: A guy named Chickie jumped him. Chickie lived on our block and we used to tease him—"Chicken Chickie!" and then we'd make chicken noises—but that was when we were seven, so he would only chase us. Danny was in the hospital for months. He came out with a giant scar, and for the rest of his life he went to work every morning at 5:30 a.m. carrying a lead pipe in his hand.

Danny hired this old lady named Mary to watch the store when he wasn't there, and whenever that happened, word would spread through the neighborhood like wildfire: "Mary's on by herself." Down the street, one kid to another would whisper: "Mary's there." Mary was not particularly good at watching the store, so it was essentially the same thing as his leaving the place unattended.

If you weren't in school when you heard that Mary was on duty by herself, you were there at the candy store in minutes, shoving fistfuls of Tootsie Rolls in your pockets. It was understood throughout Park Slope that if you couldn't steal a week's worth of Twizzlers and Wax Lips when Mary was on by herself, you didn't deserve to live in Brooklyn. Candy was everything. Mary Janes. Buttons. Sugar Babies. Bubble gum cigars. Wax with flavored water. Bit-O-Honeys. Dumb Teaberry gum. Horrible. Tea-flavored gum. Stupid. Good & Plentys, which were awful. Sugar Daddys. Turkish Taffy annoyed me, I'm not sure why. Smarties. You would buy candy and stand outside and chew it. A good piece of candy to a kid was like a glass of wine after work for an adult. You'd just feel that relaxation all over your body. *Aaaah.* It was word of mouth. You'd tell another kid. You've got to try Fruit Stripe gum. It's got a full-bodied taste that you don't find with Bazooka.

The store owners were all different, but they always treated you like an adult: "Come on, come on. Whaddya want?"

They all lived behind the store. In the back or upstairs. People would go to watch these guys get mad. They all had various degrees of anger and irritability. And when you're little, nothing's funnier than an adult losing it. I'll never forget when the guy from Pergola's meat market or the fish market got into a fight with some teenager and the kid knocked over a display or something and so he came running out with a baseball bat. And it changed the way I saw him. Before that, I thought "He's an old bald bastard," but now I was like, "Hey, this guy's ready to kill over a display! I better be nice when I come in."

That was by us. The candy stores on Fifth Avenue were a little shadier.

There were a couple of candy stores I went into where you realized, "Oh, this is a candy store with no candy." It was either a mob place or a drug place. When I was a teenager I bought drugs in a couple of those bulletproof-glass, five-year-old-items candy stores.

That's why it's sad today, when everything is a chain store. People say "name recognition" is key now. We had real name recognition: Danny, Greasy Jack, Cheap Andy. Or ethnicity: The Greek's. The Polish deli. The German bakery for cake. Not the Italian bakery—"Only go there for bread."

But even by the time I was growing up in Park Slope, many members of these white groups had fled to the suburbs, and black families had taken their place. One was the Shanks family. That was their real name. They had the one gay brother, and the other two guys were always coming back from jail ripped—and this was before jails had weight rooms, so you knew they came by those muscles using human beings as exercise equipment.

The other family—we'll call them the Smiths so we don't get sued—probably had eleven kids, a couple of cousins, and a random uncle or stepbrother, all packed into about seven rooms of a railroad flat with dirt floors. Actual dirt floors. In Park Slope. In 1974. In my neighborhood. And, of course, we were nice kids, so during fights we would tell them to go home and "water their floors" or "rake the rug."

They had a cousin who was very dark and who they called Burnt Toast. Burnt Toast, who was my age, came back from his grandma's one summer and I told him how boring that must have been. "What'd you do all day?" I asked. That was a mistake. He replied: "Every day we'd go down to the creek and one guy would get behind another guy and start fucking him in the ass and he'd get behind another and start fucking him in the ass and he'd get behind the last guy and start fucking him in the ass."

I sat there in shock, as you are doing now. I don't know if he was telling the truth or not, but I let the image wash over me, much as the waters of whatever creek they were in washed these little satyrs as they indulged in the unholy trinity of incest, buggery, and ecstasy. I pictured a Dantesque waterway adorned with the indigenous fauna and flora of the mid-Atlantic. The late summer illumination. I pictured a choreographed Jackson 5 configuration in the sickening late summer illumination, pornography by a literal light in August.

* * *

I was the only white kid on the basketball team. So I gave myself street cred and a ghetto pass. I was one of the first wiggers. Now, I know today some (all) people find that term offensive, but if you saw me in my African nationalist red, black, and green sweatbands and floppy socks, you wouldn't know what else to call it.

But as we grew older, suddenly blacks started to hang out in all-black groups and whites in all-white groups. I'm thinking of my basketball teammate Trevor, who had a no-look pass that I would try to imitate. We were close. Then one day, all of a sudden, he was wearing a dashiki and we were barely nodding acquaintances. I thought, *You used to sleep over my house.* "Ain't this a bitch," I said to myself, in a black dialect.

There is a spectrum of black comfort in white society.

1. **Likes white people better.** It's the only black guy at the Bruce Springsteen concert now that Clarence Clemons is dead. They've made their decision and they don't care.

2. **Goes both ways.** It's like how Obama can be Barry and Barack. He can like both Jay Z and Kelly Clarkson, basketball and golf.

3. **#TeamBreezy.** They have very little to do with white people. They don't care that Chris Brown battered Rihanna. They say, "Good as he look, he can hit me anytime," horrifying the white community and terrifying half the black community as well.

White people are desperate for black people's approval. The people you hate the most are the ones who love you the most, like your parents. Black people hate white people more than any other group, and yet we are your biggest fans!

The races are like America's children. White people are the firstborn, so they were Dad's favorite. Black people are the second kids, the abused ones, so they still hate Dad. Latinos are the third, caught in the middle and always trying to make peace between the other siblings. Asians are the youngest and get good marks in school but basically are just trying to keep their heads down and not get involved. And Native Americans are the old uncle who owned a house and everyone else in the family was like, "He's not using that! Let's move in!"

* * *

It seemed superfluous when we were at I.S. 88. We were called into a black-appreciation assembly for Black History Month, a tradition that debuted when I was in junior high.

We filed into the auditorium, trying to see some side-tit, which was blessedly plentiful thanks to early-seventies fashion. The dean of our grade got up and yelled that there would be consequences for any fighting, cursing, candy eating, or littering. Then the program started.

First, the one black nerd in school would get up and angrily read a Langston Hughes poem. Then we witnessed an empty stage made dramatic by the sound of offstage drums. Three black girls—two hotties and a big girl who was the terror of the girls' bathroom, forever clutching a menthol cigarette in one hand and a fistful of some blonde girl's hair in the other—entered, gyrating to "Soul Makossa" or another drum-heavy seventies African song. When their dance was over, out came the most popular black dude in school. He opened by saying, "This next song is about me." He danced by himself to Curtis Mayfield's "Superfly."

The audience screamed, fought, littered, and cursed.

Yo, that's your ego. That's your ego, yo.
Yo, I don't even fuck with the C train.
That hat-wearing motherfucker.
He don't know me, but he need to.

* * *

Black people have a problem with the System. That's why, like Eskimos for snow, they had fifty names for it, including "the Man," "Whitey," "these crackers," "Mr. Charlie," and "they" (as in, "You know how they do").

"Is the train on time?" I'll ask a black guy at the station.

"Supposed to be," he'll say with a shrug, as if he'll believe it when he sees it.

Black people don't like the fact that we're a nation of laws they didn't have a hand in writing. And so they'll make a statement with something like jaywalking. Fastest people on the planet, takes them a half hour to cross the street.

All the black people I know have conspiracy on their minds. They don't trust us. They think we photoshop everything. If you show somebody a picture of some liquid on Mars, they go "C'mon man, you don't believe that's real do you? That looks like Stone Mountain, Georgia. I was stationed near there back when I was in the service. Shit. That's Stone Mountain, Georgia. They cropped that picture."

White cops, black kids—the age-old conflict. They've been at each other for so long they've started to assume each other's traits. White cops talk like inner-city black people: "Yo, my man! What you doin'? You chillin'? Where's your homeboy?" "I ain't sweatin' you, I need to know where your hustlas at, where your ballers at, playa? Where the squad at tonight?" And black kids talk like cops: "That's a 511! That's a Class D misdemeanor! He gonna release him on recog. He ain't gonna run the plate. He lookin' at the VIN number. He from Emergency Response. That's the citywide task force. He got him on a violation. Condition unfounded. He don't need a warrant because it's in plain sight. He gotta call to Command. 10-22. That's criminal mischief.

He gonna write it up as 'refused medical attention.' He checking for priors right now. He got a outstanding bench warrant. He absconded. They gonna remand him. That's 527.6 in the penal code. Section 249. Nah, he ain't get out. That's the lieutenant. Yo, LT! The lieutenant's making the sergeant get out of the car first! He gonna request investigator. 'Cause he can't transport him to the hospital without a supervisor signing off on it."

* * *

A lot of the black girls were cute, and I liked this one girl in my class, but we were never able to get past the fact that I was funny and she wasn't shy about calling out the fact that I liked her. The black girls weren't shy. They couldn't afford to be. They had to stand up to the brothers. They had to hold their own against these black dudes that would be analyzing their every move. Not just sexually, psychologically. Black guys like to lean back and assess people. They have something to say about everything. "He short, so he has a little-man complex." "He pretty, so he act hard." "He can't dance, so he carries a gun and shoots up the club as soon as the music starts so no one can ever find out."

And women. Men in every ethnic group have their own relationship with women. The Italians and Puerto Ricans are trying to bang half and make the other half mommy them, the Jews are trying to stand up to them, but the black guys have a whole psychological thing that they're just always trying to provoke them. They're trying to annoy and charm at the same time. They like to argue with women. I'd go to any city agency and there's a lady behind the counter arguing with a black guy in line and they're not even looking at each other.

THE GUY: "Some people get a little power and they want to abuse people but that's alright."

THE LADY: "And some people think they can come in like they deserve special treatment but they don't. They got to wait like everybody else."

Black guys think they're experts on women. "She wear too much mascara. That means she likes light-skinned brothers." Or "Her fingernails are cracked. That means she has more than two kids." Or "She got too many toe rings. That means she only goes with Colombians."

Black guys are always analyzing women's genetic makeup. They're like walking DNA test kits: "Damn, look at that ass! She about 40 percent Brazilian... She Honduran on her father side... Ooh, Indian and part Chinese!"

They like exotic flavor combinations in their food, too. When a train I'm on stops near a black high school, three hundred kids get on, each with a flavor of soda I have never heard of. There are choruses of, "Yo, kid, run me a taste of that birchberry kiwi!" "What the fuck is that, yesterday's sour hawberry tea?" "Don't steal my White Fungus Bird's Nest soda, man!"

Black guys are also the only people who seem to genuinely not mind being cheated on. They have that sexual confidence. They will say, "Shit, *tssss*, she trynna make me jealous." They never cockblock. They always want to know that somebody's "hitting that," except people didn't used to say "hitting that" or "tapping that." I think it was "getting some." If a black guy saw you with a girl and he asked, "Are you in there?" and you said no, you'd ruin his whole day. "Awww. Why not, man?" "Well, she's got a boyfriend who lives in Queens." They would stop whatever they were doing and stare in disbelief. "In Queens? He's in Queens? And she's in Brooklyn and you're in Brooklyn! What is your problem, man?"

* * *

Different races have different ideas about what's rude and what's polite. Black people will never break a date or argue about the restaurant choice. Instead, they show up three hours late, having already eaten what they wanted to.

Black customers and Arab counterpeople are like the oil and water of the deli interaction. Arabs never turn on the charm and they never blink. The black customer will say, "Yo, what kind of ham is that?"

Arab guy: "It's ham."

"But is it like that Boar's Head shit, or—"

"It's ham!"

"Okay, man. Let me get a ham on rye with..."

"Hurry up!"

"Mustard. Yo, I see you slicing that ham thin. Make sure you give me enough."

"I give you the right amount!"

But the reason there's racial tension is that groups' quirks and preferences all come out in these little social exchanges. White people back down in public but black people have no problem creating drama in public. They're not afraid to cause a scene. They don't get embarrassed. Meanwhile, you see white people so well intentioned that they wind up being racist. They hold black people to a totally different standard.

When a black girl is getting crazy in a store, white people will freeze and start backing quietly away. It's a muscle memory, this sense that, "Oh well, this is justifiable anger, even if she seems in this situation to be unreasonable." Other races don't have this same anxiety level. The Asian shopkeeper won't second-guess. He will just shout back, "Get the fuck out of my store! You go smoke crack!"

White people do exciting shit boring, and black people do boring shit exciting. We will skateboard volcanoes and base jump off a canyon but cause someone to fall asleep when we explain it to them. Black guys can do nothing all day, but when you hear them explain their day, it sounds like they've been skateboarding volcanoes.

Black people have a secret society of black artists about

whom most white people are totally oblivious. You're walking down the street looking at a long line outside a theater and it's like, "Wait, who's Janelle Monáe?" Black people know everything there is to know about the one black person on a white show who you don't even think about—some black guy from a show like *CSI* who wins six Image Awards, and we go, "What's an Image Award?"

We also have a society they don't know about. Like, they've never heard of The National or *Parks and Recreation*. Sometimes we try to bridge this gap, and when we do, look what happens. The best example is Stevie Wonder and Paul McCartney, two musical masters of the twentieth century. In the mid-eighties, they decided to help the racial dialogue by getting together and composing a song. They came up with "Ebony and Ivory," one of the worst songs ever written. It makes you think maybe Mark David Chapman did John Lennon a favor, so he didn't have to live through that abomination.

* * *

We could teach a course in how not to have a conversation. Every conversation about race consists of saying we need to have a conversation about race and everyone nodding their head solemnly. "Yes, race is a complicated issue," someone will say sagely. "Yes, race is tricky," another will say, followed by a few more generalizations. We hate generalizations in our society unless they are about generalizing. Why? Well, one reason is because people get used to saying the same things and it's comfortable. Here's how it goes:

A Shooting of a Black Kid by a White Cop...

The black people start screaming...

The white people start stammering...

Some behind-the-scenes activities with the Sharptons of the world and the attorney general or the mayor or whoever...

People make pronouncements about retraining police, changing systemic ingrained attitudes...

The cops are the proxy for the system...

Finally things calm down on their own and everybody breathes a sigh of relief...

Until the next time...

Black people—you showed us the shadow side of the American Dream. We appreciate that. You made us look at the parts of our personality we didn't want to see. Thanks. We get it. Now quit acting like just because we did you evil you are saints.

A lot of my black friends have said, "White people are responsible for all the evil in the world." That's considered a sophisticated narrative and viewpoint. A lot of white people feel the same way. I'm not going to say we don't have a big responsibility for the bad, as we have been in charge of a large part of the world for a long time. But there are percentages. There's no way 100 percent of the evil is on us.

How about we take 80 percent? Are you telling me that all white society is evil and all black society is good? How about 20 percent of your problems you take for yourselves? You committed heinous atrocities in America and Africa, too. You broke Detroit. You can't completely blame the school system for your kids failing when you're bringing them to a midnight showing of *Saw 7*. Quit saying that you will handle your community problems yourselves. You're taking too long. Either we're in this together or we're not. If you have any questions or complaints, come to me and me only. I will handle it for you.

II

Muscle Car Chrome

In 1975, I was in high school in Bensonhurst, which was all Italian. And I mean all Italian. Those were the days of the second Italian Renaissance, when they ran their parts of Brooklyn like a separate city.

Up and down the block, Italian guys would be washing cars while their fathers heckled them from their stoops, yelling, "Check the alternator! You're holding that hose like it's your prick, ya fuckin' meatball!" The kid would mutter to himself and continue spraying, while the father would comment to his neighbor, "This kid don't know how to wash a fuckin' car; he don't even know how to wash his ass" or some other family non-therapeutically approved remark.

Every once in a while, one of them would call you over and say, "Let me tell you a secret." You'd have to walk across the street, out of your way, and then they'd lean in and whisper, "The Mets have no pitchers this year." But they'd have no problem yelling something down the street that actually should have been a secret: "Ey, just put a little topical ointment on. It'll clear up in two days!" And their linguistics would make seemingly innocuous questions sound threatening: "Beautiful day today—right or wrong?"

When Italians like you, they make you feel like the most important person in the world just arrived. They literally start yelling at any other person there and get in a fight because they're not being hospitable enough to you.

"What's the matter with you? You don't get the guy a drink of water? He's sitting here like a *jadrool*. Give the guy a drink of something."

The gods were Tony Danza, John Travolta, Robert De Niro, and Sylvester Stallone. Disco became a big thing after *Saturday Night Fever*, and Italians, also known back then as "hitters," had a real knack for it...and for hitting, by the way. They weren't into working out before the movie *Rocky*. But within months of that film coming out, every Italian kid was doing one-arm push-ups in front of our high school.

This wasn't a great thing for us Irish guys. Suddenly, the Irish and Jews were forced to work out, too. Irish guys are supposed to be fat, or skinny with a fat gut. Those are our looks. Back in the fifties, those were good times for us. Your body didn't matter. Look at Frank Sinatra. Nobody cared that he had a paunch. Sean Connery? Fat. But you were covered up. Men got away with murder. Women just had to have big tits. Nobody looked at their asses. You could have no ass or a flat ass or a fat ass; it was irrelevant until everyone started wearing jeans in 1967.

Then came this *mamaluke*—Sylvester Stallone. This fool decided to get in shape for *Rocky*. He ruined it for everyone. Paul Newman, when he played a boxer, did he get in shape? No, he basically just wore a shirt with the name of his character on it. And now, because of Sly's stupid work ethic, I had to go to the gym, where trainers invent all these great exercises no one can do.

Italians were very openly sexual. Let me amend that: The guys were. The girls were not allowed to be. Italian girls had to roll their eyes and stir the gravy in front of their family. They had to act like virgins, even though it was the seventies and virginity was over. They had to act like the girl Al Pacino marries in Sicily in *The Godfather*—"beautiful... but virtuous."

The only way they were allowed to act out their sexuality was in their clothes. Italian girls were allowed to wear the tightest, most provocative clothes, and that was somehow fine with their parents. They would show up at high school and you could see all the male teachers trying not to look at those Jordache jeans asses bouncing by. The girls were allowed to dress like that because they were usually accompanied by the boys, who were also wearing tight designer jeans, disco shirts, and marshmallow shoes.

Italians are scared of the wrong things. They will rush

into a gang fight. But if you hand them a Greek yogurt, "Yeah," they say, looking at it like it's a bomb about to go off, "but are you sure it don't get you sick?"

Italians would put their seat back as far as it could go, only driving with one hand. To put two hands on the wheel was considered unmasculine. Holding your dick when you pissed was considered unmasculine. I swear to God, my Italian friend was pissing next to me one time at a urinal and he lectured me about how I shouldn't be holding my dick, I guess because it's gay to hold a dick for too long even if it's your own. But for being such tough guys, they were awfully physical and emotionally intimate with other men: hugging, kissing, pinching, grabbing your face, close-talking, ass-slapping. They wore their hearts on their sleeves, even though they never wore sleeves.

They were touchers. Always touching you. I don't know if that's how they could tell you were listening or how they decided if they could trust you, by how you reacted, but they would always talk to you with an accompanying grab or touch.

"How you doin'? Good?" Then they grab your hip.

"How's your family?" Then they grab your arm.

"You're looking good, ya bastard." Then they lightly punch you in the stomach and they'd touch their own hands.

Always with the hands. They'd tell you a story and explain that they weren't there to cause trouble—"...my hand to God"—and they'd put their hand over their heart and look you in the eye till you nodded. Or they'd show how they had to pay the guy off by wiping one palm above the other palm. They always had to pay somebody off. Whoever they were dealing with had to be taken care of. Money was always exchanging hands, and they were always tipping heavily. Occasionally, there was a frugal Italian and they'd talk about him: "He's a fuckin' miser; he don't go for spit, that penny pincher bastard." To Italians, the worst thing you could be is somebody who didn't like to spend money.

And it was always cash. Every Italian male over thirty had a pocketful of cash. They would pull it out and ask you if you needed anything. That was their way of saying "I love you." They were saying, "If you need cash, I'm actually willing to give it to you right now." Most people live in fear of someone asking them if they have any money. These guys were actively telling you that they have money and all you have to do is ask for it.

They all kept baseball bats in their cars. I saw plenty of Italians in action around places like 86th Street or Avenue U back in the seventies. They'd be chatting, stopped at a light, with guys on the corner, and then some guy would honk and the guy leaning into the car would say, "Cool your jets, scumbag!" Then the other guy would get out of the car and go, "Did you just call me a scumbag, douchebag?" And then they would start beating the shit out of each other. Or they would both reach in and grab bats and then it would be a standoff.

Nobody ever hit the other guy with the bat, and certainly nobody hit the other guy's *car* with the bat, because they knew it would be death if they did. And you knew the leaning guy would probably be switching positions with the honking guy next week.

Everything that Italians did in Brooklyn back then revolved around their cars. They met girls by pulling up alongside them in their car. They got into fights because someone touched their car. They spent hours inspecting or cleaning their car. They had weapons strategically placed in their car. They would take pictures of their car. They would take pictures of their girlfriend on top of their car.

So you had these blocks all over the borough, with daughters stopping traffic and sons washing cars and husbands flashing cash and wives yelling out windows and kids playing in the street. It all started to look like it could've been some little village in Sicily, because it was one: a little place where the clotheslines were being pulled in and the guys were wearing the wife-beaters and their hands were gesturing with their cigarettes and their plotting. Italians love to ruminate, always stewing about what some enemy was up to and strategizing how they were gonna pay him back—"That piece of shit Mario, wait'll I see him"—and then they'd all go out and parade down the avenue.

People say the Irish love a parade. We do it once a year. The Italians would do it every Friday night down 86th Street. They'd come in from Staten Island and Queens to the old country, Brooklyn, and they'd be leaning out of their cars blasting disco music and talking to girls. It was one of those lost New York things that everybody knew about but nobody thought twice of. It was just a Friday night fact, but now it's gone and nobody filmed it.

* * *

On my old block lived an ex-boxer nicknamed Joey Savage. All day, he would just lean out the window in his wife-beater and threaten his son, my friend Paulie. Joey Savage was Dr. Phil's worst nightmare: "Paulie, ya fuckin' idiot, get outta the street!" he would yell. "You're gonna get hit by a car, ya fuckin' moron!"

This was a man who went by the name Joey Savage, so I guess he couldn't be expected to lean out the window and yell, "Paulie! I love you, but I express my anxiety in the aggressive way in which I was brought up to express such uncomfortable feelings! I masquerade my pain and fear for you by calling you a fucking moron even though you're an intelligent and sensitive person and I love you!" And it was just the way the Italian culture worked. They had fifty names for moron: *stunadz, chooch, sfaccim, cafon, giamoke, mamaluke*...If you worked hard enough, appraisal of your stupidity could get reduced to "half a fucking momo."

An Irish family like mine would wait till they went inside to shame their children through gritted teeth: "How dare you? How fuckin' dare you speak to your mother like that? In the middle of the street. Trying to be clever in front of your friends?" I get it today from my Irish relatives. Just the other day, I told my cousin Tim Gage that I was going to appear at a George Carlin event, and he said, in a deflating tone perfected by generations of our shame-inducing ancestors, "Why'd they pick *you*?"

Paulie had a cousin, Donna, who was slow but pretty hot. Of course, before any of us could process that thought, a nineteen-year-old Puerto Rican kid from Sunset Park had knocked her up. With Puerto Ricans around, you either make your move fast, or you're out. You can't think that just because a girl's a little heavy you won't have plenty of competition for her. There's a line in Spanish I heard often: "Que frondosa tehuantepec." That means, "How fat and luxuriant you are."

Don't try to pick up a white girl by saying that. If you get away without a drink thrown in your face, good for you. But you can actually get away with—really, get pretty far—calling a Spanish girl some poetic variation on "big." It's not a bad thing in those cultures. The Puerto Ricans like a few pounds. The Dominicans like a big ass and big legs. Mexicans like all that, plus a gut.

This Mafia loan shark who lived in the neighborhood would stand outside and yell at us all day—things that sounded sort of like threats and sort of like promises and sort of like compliments: "What is it, killaaaah?" Or "We gotta get the Detroit mob after ya!"

He got robbed at gunpoint by these two guys. They handcuffed him to the door handle of his Cadillac. His wife came out and saw her husband attached to the car, shaking, having survived a brush with death. She yelled, "Somebody call the *New York Post* so we get a picture!"

Their son was a dope fiend. He would get high in his car in front of the house and then go on the nod. Every night, around 1 a.m., if I was awake, I would go out and knock on his car window. He would look at me bleary-eyed, mutter "Thanks," and stumble into the house. It was the gentle nudge that he never got from his old man, who was distracted by chasing women and compulsive gamblers.

When my parents got divorced, the loan shark asked my mother out right in front of his own wife. He hollered at my mom across the street, "Hey, Red!" (She has red hair.) "When are you gonna let me take you out for a steak dinner?"

Yeah, that would have been the best way to offset the trauma of my parents' divorce: having my mother become the *goomata* of a low-level bookie for the Colombos.

* * *

I was seeing quite enough of the Mafia on my own time. One day, someone cordially invited me to a sweet sixteen party at the Palm Shore Club, one of those Italian Mafia–run dinner-and-show places in Sheepshead Bay, Brooklyn. (Now the Russian Mafia owns these clubs, so you feel a little bit more Continental when they give you the old Viggo Mortensen to the chops.)

The club was a one-room-fits-all-events-type space. So it was a sweet sixteen at three tables, next to an office retirement, next to a guy that just got his gold shield, next to a guy who just got out of jail. And in the middle was a stage with performances. I can't imagine anyone voluntarily choosing to do this gig. I suspect it was probably more of a Russell-Crowe-in-*Gladiator* situation—they would just throw you up there and point spears at you if you tried to leave. But there I was with a bunch of my friends and a bunch of these other guys who lived in their buildings.

So a couple of my friends and I decided to drop acid. I had smoked a lot of pot and done other drugs and drank but never done acid before. The thing with acid is you always think it's not working until it starts to work, and by then you've let your guard down and you are in too deep and then it's like being dragged along on a sled for eight hours.

There was a girl there named Gwenn, and I was in love with her. She lived in the Luna Park public housing by the Coney Island amusement park. Back then, all of that part of Brooklyn was full of blue-collar Jews: places like Trump Village, Luna Park, and Sheepshead Bay. That's where Andrew Dice Clay is from. These were the Jewish kids who grew up poor and didn't go to temple. Lots of taxi drivers lived there.

Gwenn was a petite, fifteen-year-old rocker who was considered "moody." She was not afraid to fight, and she had me incorrectly pegged as a world-class badass, because the first time I went to her house I got into a fight with some other young fellow.

Well, we start to trip. Everything is just grand. I'm stoned and everybody else seems stoned. Then Gwenn comes up to me and points to one of the other sweet-sixteeners and says, "That guy sold me and my friends weak pot. We aren't stoned at all."

Well, I saw my opportunity to rush to the maiden's rescue, and I was grateful for the chance to prove myself. She was everything to me, and I hadn't even kissed her yet.

I go over to their side of the table and lean down in my denim jacket, and I whisper to the dealer of the beat weed and all his friends who are listening and wondering what this interloper wants, "Hey, man, we got a little problem. The girl says you sold her a light bag."

This guy looks at me and says, "No I didn't." Then he turns his head around and starts talking to his friends. Dismissed. He acted like I wasn't even there.

Little did he realize that I was so in love with this girl that if she had told me she was being sexually harassed by a lion, I would've gone to the zoo and crawled into the cage and put my hand on the lion's mane and said, "The lady's not interested, man, so give it up!" I was that very lethal combination of being in love and having no identity.

When this guy dismissed me, he neglected to take into account my lack of options. I had nowhere to go. I pulled my best sly rap move. I laughed and shook my head like I was leaving and then turned back into him with a nice shot right to the old side of the head, followed by the old quick-drag backward, off his chair onto the floor. Followed by all his friends on top of me.

In the ensuing melee, the birthday girl's grandmother kicked me in my ear so hard it became caked with blood. (I only have partial hearing in that ear to this day.) And then I was dragged away by a couple of Mafia goons who worked for the Palm Shore.

The last thing I saw before being pulled out of the hall was the performer in the middle of the room. He was an old Catskills comedian onstage, and he was pleading with us in a desperate fashion. "Come on, fellas," he was saying uneasily. "Everyone calm down."

That poor guy. I totally ruined his set. He's haunted me ever since. Every time since then that I've been onstage when a fight's broken out in the audience, I've felt that pitiful guy's spirit looking down at me, saying, "*You* recover from this, asshole."

The two furious Mafia princes took me into the basement and beat the shit out of me. Here I was, the last gallant man, tripping, being subjected to body blow after body blow. The situation could've easily ended up with me being found in the back of a butcher truck while "Layla" played in the background, but I guess there were too many witnesses. And they could tell from my explanation that my only problem was that I was hopelessly pussy whipped.

Finally, they helped me out the door with a couple of nice combinations to the cranium and left me to find my friends, who as soon as the coast was clear appeared from around the corner of the building, laughing. The rest of the night was spent in true acid fun—feeling five minutes ahead of where you just were and then three hours behind, and trying not to kill yourself, and then repeating the process.

Gwenn and I wound up dating for a few years after that. In each other's company, we were turtledoves. Separately, we were each more like Sid without Nancy. More than once, we wound up in various legal predicaments. She was cursing someone out at one end of town, and I would be nursing a couple of egg-shaped lumps at central booking on the other. The world was a safer place when we were together.

* * *

One of my first bartending jobs was in one of these Italian places, in Bay Ridge. You walk in and think to yourself, "Hmmm, why does that maître d' with bricklayer hands have six rings on his finger? Why is no one looking at the coat check girl's tits? Why is the sous-chef missing a pinkie?" You walk in and 90 percent of the people in the place are not waiters or bartenders or customers but another mysterious category of people who are never to be charged for drinks. They are pseudo-employed there, only they do no work, and the boss only gives you the guy's relative's name as his job description.

"Who's that?" I'd ask.

"That's Frank's brother."

"Oh, okay."

"Who's that?"

"He's with Carmine."

"Okay."

Never mind that you don't know who this guy is or what he does—you don't even know who Carmine is. But you know one thing: If you were ever to say, "Hey, by the way, who's Carmine?" you would quickly find your scent being hosed out of Henry Hill's trunk while he tells his wife he hit a skunk.

You are expected to know all these guys because the Italian mob in Brooklyn back then were all convinced they were famous. It was acceptable to not know him personally, but you had to at least say you "know *of* him."

The other tip-off that this was a mob joint was that the manager would make you push a different beer and liquor every night. Whatever came in, that's what you'd sell: "Tell them we only got Michelob Light in cans and a very nice Cuban scotch."

The main bartender, Paul, thought my name was Collins the whole time I worked there. He was also one of those guys who thought that if you said anything at all that he didn't understand, that made you either stupid or crazy.

"I'm starting to do a little stand-up comedy," I told Paul.

"You're a fuckin' joke to begin with!"

He was very proud of himself for coming up with that, and so he repeated his crack to people all day, like it was an Oscar Wilde quote instead of the simplistic musing of a total ass, calculated to crush dreams. "Hey, did you hear what

I told Collins here? He told me, 'I'm gonna be a comedian,' and I told him, 'You're already a joke anyways!' "

One waiter there was a guy I didn't get along with at all. He was abrasive, in my opinion, although I was certainly not employee of the year either. One night we ended up fighting on Third Avenue, rolling over a car as we grappled. Amid curses and threats, our coworkers broke it up. I took a car service home, secure in the knowledge that I was a good man who'd just been pushed too far.

The next day, I was informed that the guy I'd fought was related to the owners, and that it was unfortunate I had chosen him for my nemesis. As it turned out, I was in rather a great deal of trouble. Management wished to talk to me "off-site."

Now, I wasn't the most street-smart fellow in Brooklyn, but I certainly knew that if I showed up at whatever predetermined social club hosted the personnel department that day, it was going to end with me receiving a subpar performance evaluation in the form of a trip to Lutheran Hospital.

Unlike the Pope of Greenwich Village, who in that movie goes and boldly confronts the boss, I kept a low profile. In fact, from then on I kept entirely out of Bay Ridge except to visit my lovely grandma. And I sought employment elsewhere, with different Italians.

* * *

I had to deal with another Italian crew when I worked at a health club on Kings Highway in Brooklyn. The gym was next to the car service with no cars and the candy store with no candy. Guys would use the gym on a payment plan that allowed them to quit at any time. This made sense for them. If you get locked up, you don't want to be paying for a gym that you won't get to use for eight to twelve years.

Most of the guys were friendly, considering, though they never learned my name and always called me "Irish." They wouldn't pay their dues, but they would still complain about shit all the time: "Hey, Irish, the whirlpool's not working again. What kind of rip-off place is this?" Always, they were threatening to take their nonbusiness to another club.

The manager, a dummy named Eric, who hated me and didn't realize that a bunch of fifty-year-old muscle men who had nothing to do every afternoon might possibly be involved in illicit activities, goes to me, "Listen, from now on, I want you to check everybody's cards when they come in. If they owe money, you say you are holding the card until they pay."

"Let me get this straight," I said. "I tell them they have to pay me money. I then refuse to give them something they handed to me, something that is probably their only noncounterfeit form of ID. What's more, this ID has their picture on it, which is probably the only current picture of them, and therefore something that the Feds would love to have. And then I tell them I am not going to give it back to them until they pay me money. So, basically, you want me to blackmail a bunch of mobsters."

I don't know much about mobsters, but from what I do know, they don't react well to ultimatums. Nor do they seem comfortable being called on their character flaws. They don't appear to be malleable or to be particularly motivated to discover their own culpability when a situation goes wrong. I wouldn't say their first instinct is to weigh the merits of the other person's argument.

So I finally go up to one of the guys who owed money and say, "They want you to pay up. I'm supposed to keep your card. Gimme the card."

"No," he said.

"Okay," I said.

Eric asked me, "Did you tell him to pay?"

"Yes," I said.

"Did you keep his card?"

"No."

"Why not?"

"Well... This is a health club. He told me it would be bad for my health."

Intentionally, I had gone to the one guy who had a shred of humanity. He was the only one who didn't have those pupils that had stared down the dark hallways of too many penitentiaries. This guy was the talker. Still a killer, but he was the personality guy who would talk until he came up with a good sound bite. You were always lucky that you came to him.

"Lucky you came to me. If you went to Louie with this... he would've..."

Then he does the look around, to find whatever could be a weapon, depending on the physical location. If it's a drugstore, you'd get the crutch. A TV repair store, you'd get the antennae, etc.

"I mean, Louie would've hit you with a thirty-five-pound weight. He would've drowned you in the hot tub. He would've cracked you with the curl bar. He would've choked you with a towel." But this guy knew that this was not my fault; it was the corporation. These were the early days of franchises and I had just received one of the benefits: You could blame an invisible force. Since there was no one to shake down, I got a "pass" and went on to have a long, happy career there (I got fired two weeks later for drinking on my lunch break).

* * *

In seventies Brooklyn, an Italian rocker-stoner subculture flourished. Guys like the Ramones. They were the brothers in the family who didn't like disco. My Italian friend Richie and I were tripping one time in Bath Beach. He was smiling and talking away and I was trying hard to figure out what he was saying. Finally I realized he was singing me the Beatles song "Martha My Dear." There's nothing more incongruous than a cold, windy day, tripping on Bay 50th Street and a big Italian starts not singing but reciting "Martha My Dear" to you. Then we went back to class and Richie tried to answer a question but ended up rambling, putting words together that had never been together before.

He ended up laughing and crying at the same time. The teacher just rolled her eyes and went back to teaching.

Acid was a big deal, but pot was bigger. We all dealt weed at various times, and we all bought it from each other. The Italians loved pot, and this was before coke. But they couldn't let their fathers find out or else they'd really get a beating. Everybody else was allowed to smoke pot, but not the Italians. Their parents were old-fashioned. They hated, on principle, what pot stood for in America. They were very patriotic. They were the ones that were marching down in hard hats to beat up the hippies. They all had flags on their houses. Some Irish were old-fashioned, too, but any touching, heart-swelling sincerity, in any form, was immediately mocked. They'd get the smirk when anybody said something sincere. "Aren't you a great American?" And, "How touching that you let us all know you love this country."

One teacher moved to my neighborhood and bumped into me in the street one day and after a quick hello asked me who around here might be "holding." But there were also real pot dealers who did it for a living and who you would go see when nobody you knew had good product. These pot dealers were all the same: dirtbags with a little bit of hippie in them.

There was a code of etiquette: You weren't just able to buy the smoke and leave. First you had to burn a couple of joints with them. You had to hang out with them for a couple of hours at every transaction, just to make sure they trusted you and because part of the reason they dealt drugs was so that people would have to hang out with them, as on their own they were not too successful with interpersonal relationships.

I knew quite a few of these characters, because I smoked a lot, and I would subcontract myself out to buy for other people for a small commission. So one time I go to see a guy whose name I can't remember. I guarantee it was something ridiculous. All of the drug dealers had nicknames ending in "-man": Pipeman, Ganjaman, Chibaman, Toastman. Let's call this particular guy Blubberman. He was Italian, and kind of a fat bastard.

So I went to his house. We never really liked each other, but I think he knew that I wielded enough clout that if he chose not to deal to me, he would have to tell other people why, and he couldn't say he didn't trust me, because I was well known as a trustworthy type. If he were to cut me off, he would have to publicly admit he just didn't like me and then explain why—except that you can't explain why you don't like someone unless it's someone everybody hates, and unfortunately for him, I was not universally hated.

And even if he had tried to say that I was a prick, everybody would still have said, "A prick should still be allowed to buy pot." Because that's how it was in those days: Pot buying was seen as an inalienable right. But okay, so this guy didn't like me, and I didn't like him. I thought he was a fat bore. Every time I came in there he was listening to either Jeff Beck or John McLaughlin or some other guitarist that you weren't allowed to not like.

Plus, whenever I went over there with a girl, he would try to let her know that anytime she wanted to come back on her own, it was cool. Then he would smile with his little Chiclet teeth and say, "I mean, you know where I live now, right?" like it was a brilliant witticism.

I'd go over to his house on Dahill Road in Brooklyn. He lived in the back of a building and I'd ring the bell. His mother would let me in. I'm not sure if she was so blinded by love of her child that she looked at this urine-smelling lump and saw the homecoming king, or if she knew and was proud that he was slinging ganja out of the house and was cut in on the profits.

So this one day I showed up with a girl I liked quite a bit, and this was our first date—go buy pot, then get high at her house, listen to some Hot Tuna, and dry hump until our jeans caught fire. That was my plan, anyway. But I brought her in, and right away I notice Blubberman starts giving her the dissertation about the various assholes he deals pot to.

And then I realized this pimple wizard was describing someone unnervingly similar to me. Well, although I was never in the top rankings fight-wise, I was under the mistaken impression that I was pretty "handy," and I knew that I could beat the living balls out of this jerk. But I didn't do anything about it that day.

The girl and I took a desultory train ride home and didn't talk much after that. But I couldn't help stewing, and a couple of months later I went back to Blubberman's house and climbed in his window, thinking I would grab some pot to make us even. Fatso and his mother came in and they both grabbed me. Blubberman had me under his awful sweating body in his stupid *ZigZag* magazine T-shirt, and the mother was scratching my face. We ended up on a floor covered in bong water. To escape, I had to pinch his fat arm and punch him in the elbow. I ran down the street with them screaming bloody murder after me.

Then I had to lie to the friends who originally had turned me on to Blubberman about what caused the fight. I told them that his mother was trying to have sex with me and then Blubberman came home and saw us and bugged out. I had everybody believing me except my one friend who said, "Bullshit. You were probably trying to rob his pot like he said." And at that, everybody kind of nodded their heads, like, "Yeah. That makes more sense."

* * *

Goodfellas and *Taxi Driver* are the movies that are New York. Before *27 Dresses*, of course. So I always knew I had a connection with Robert De Niro, the Italian king of film. I always secretly felt that if De Niro ever got to spend some time with me, he'd be like, "Where has this guy been hiding?" Keitel's out, Quinn's in.

So it seemed like destiny when one day eleven years ago, Robert De Niro's wife called me and said she was having a surprise party for him. "Would you come and do a quick De Niro impression at the restaurant?" she asked.

One thing you learn after years in show business is that a birthday party at a restaurant is a classic hell gig. People want to eat and talk. The last thing they want to do is to listen to you. *But this is different*, I think, *because it's De Niro, it's Scorsese—my people.*

Then I started preparing for the gig. Usually I wouldn't write twenty minutes of new material for a two-minute impression. I sat home for three nights in a row and wrote a whole new three-part set. Part one was me coming out and zinging people with quick ones, like a roast, boom, get a few laughs. Part two, I was planning to tell a humorous but moving story about the first time I heard about De Niro. And then the third part was going to be me doing scenes from De Niro's movies. This was the natural order of what I'd been working toward.

I was bursting with confidence. I had just reached the point of my career where I felt like I had really figured it all out. I was so tight onstage. I knew exactly what I was doing. That I had been called for this gig at this exact moment seemed like it was meant to be.

So I get to the gig. I look out at the audience. At one table sit Whoopi Goldberg, Robin Williams, and Billy Crystal—other comics to appreciate my artistry.

De Niro's wife offers to introduce me, and I say I don't need an introduction. Not with this act. I'll just walk out onstage while everyone is eating the first course and start talking. *It will be more organic that way.* As I stroll out and grab the mike, I notice that some people are turning to each other and whispering things like, "Who is that?" They're about to find out.

"It's great to be here," I begin. "You know, I met De Niro once very briefly..." People are starting to look uncomfortable. "You are one of the greatest actors of all time," I say, while starting to gently rib De Niro. "Do you do any other accents?"

Everyone just stared at me.

"No, seriously," I say, "you do a lot of hard work preparing for your roles. You've gained weight for *Raging Bull*, and then for *The Untouchables* you put on a few...Hey, maybe you're just a fat bastard who likes to eat."

Everyone is now looking at me like, "Who is this son of a bitch insulting De Niro on his birthday?"

"Speaking of preparation," I say. "How did you prepare for *Rocky & Bullwinkle*? By looking in the mirror and apologizing to your fans?"

It is at this point that I realize I'm only a couple of minutes in and I'm in a little bit of trouble. I look out the rain-streaked window at St. Patrick's Cathedral and say a quick prayer.

Normally, in a situation like this, a pro like myself would stop messing around and go right into his quick impression and get it over with. But I wasn't going to let this opportunity pass me by. I begin part two: my emotional De Niro story.

Now my mouth is dry. I'm saying parts of the story out of sequence, and words out of order and backward. "I mean,

De Niro seriously is great!" I hear myself saying—as if his assembled friends need me, a guy who doesn't even know him, to sign off on an American treasure.

Everyone starts looking at me with hate. Some pity. Mostly hate. And once the audience hates you, it's over. It doesn't matter what you do; you're not getting them back.

But, for some reason, I can't let myself give up my dream—this dream of being the missing ingredient of Tribeca Films. So I arrive at part three of my plan. Here I am, on the podium. Everybody hates my guts. And what do I do? I double down. Even though I am not known for my vocal range, I go into a four-person scene from *Goodfellas*, doing all the voices.

People are just mortified now. Especially De Niro's wife, whose idea all this was, is looking at me like, "Get. Off. Now." Because she's the Oppenheimer of this bomb.

My whole face is sweating from shame. And this was a room full of actors and directors, whose job it is to study faces. I felt like everyone could see inside me like an X-ray: I'm a sham. My whole life is miserable.

Finally I just said, "Seriously—Happy birthday," and I got offstage to a smattering of sarcastic applause. Even if they hate you, people can still applaud, but by the way they clap you can tell they're not saying, "Thank you." They're saying, "Thank you for ruining our party."

In front of the restaurant, I'm trying to pull myself together and get a cab, because I still had another gig that night. My one consolation was that I had an extra shirt to change into, a nice new cashmere shirt I was very proud of ($200 dollars, not that you asked). In my family, we don't carry suit bags. You just carry your extra clothes with you on a hanger, like a valet. Anyway, it was good I had the extra shirt, because the shirt under my suit was soaked through to the core with sweat.

Robin Williams, who I knew a little bit, comes outside, crying with laughter. He is laughing his balls off. "You know what my wife said when you went up onstage?" he asks me, as tears of mirth stream down his face. "'What's that guy with the microphone doing up there, Robin?' she said. 'Go up there and help him.'"

The only way this evening could have gone worse, I realize, is if Robin Williams had come up and started doing his act and the whole crowd had cried, "Thank you, Robin, for saving us!"

But I had to try to protect my ego somehow. I started to play it off. "You know, Robin," I say, feigning nonchalance, "that went badly, but it really doesn't bother me. I'm doing so many gigs, and one bomb is..."

And then Robin started laughing again, because he noticed that, while I was talking, my shirt—my exciting new cashmere shirt—had fallen off the hanger and into a puddle on the sidewalk. As I turn to get it—and I am not kidding—a cab drives by and sends up a cascade of water, completely soaking me.

And Scorsese wasn't even there.

* * *

Italians, you were a fun, colorful people, but I don't think the suburbs are your thing. It's taking the drama out of you. You need to be yelling at your husbands, or crying, or flirting, and all those things need to be done with a big audience or it gets depressing. You need to be leaning out tenement windows laughing, screeching into parking spots, and jumping out of cars while cursing. You need to be opera, not reality TV. I suggest you move back to the cities, because you're not happy where you are. I know it was the American Dream. But be careful what you wish for, right?

III

Picante Papaya

FOR A MINUTE THERE, WHEN I WAS IN MIDDLE SCHOOL, THE Latinos—in particular, Puerto Ricans—dominated New York. My friends and I all tried to dress like the Puerto Ricans. We wore six-inch heels and polka-dot shirts. Tony Orlando was popular—the band Tavares, too. Well, Tony Orlando was half Greek, and Tavares was Cape Verdean, but they were considered Puerto Rican by everybody.

Puerto Ricans are walking contradictions. On the one hand, they're religious and family oriented. On the other hand, they are hypersexualized from the age of about eleven. It's a mixed message. You'll have a car with saints hanging off the dashboard next to a decal of a naked woman. You'll have an old aunt in a sexy tube top next to a girl in a First Communion dress.

Puerto Ricans would have full-fledged relationships in

sixth grade. We would go on a class trip, and while I was looking at some dinosaur they'd be furiously making out inside a prehistoric turtle shell. There was no "Will you be my girlfriend?" No note-passing. No spin the bottle. They would be arguing over infidelity at thirteen, living together at fourteen, and parents by fifteen.

I remember this Puerto Rican kid in my elementary school, Frankie, describing having had sex with a girl in our class. Not only was I pretty sure he was lying, I didn't even know what he was talking about. Now, I know there are problems with us uptight "European Victorians," but you have to have at least some boundaries. Puerto Ricans do not agree. Boys hit on girls in front of their mothers. And the mother looks at the girl, too, like, "Well, you gonna answer my son?" They hit on any girl that walks by, even pregnant ones. To pregnant women, they call out, with zero irony, "Hey, *mami*!"

We all loved hanging out on the stoop, but Puerto Ricans raised it to an art form. The stoop-sitters would also predict the baby's sex: "Yo, that's a girl. I could tell." They were the 1970s ultrasound. "Yo, she's carrying high. That's a boy!"

Very social people. They'd sit on the stoop like the public advocate. "Yo, don't park there, you're too close to the hydrant. These cops around here will give you a ticket in a minute, these cops."

There was always one quiet kid in the family, and they'd introduce him like he had a disease—"That's Peter. He's quiet"—and then look at you like, "What can you do? It's God's will."

I spoke Spanish to the Puerto Ricans in my neighborhood. Well, not Spanish, but street Spanish, New York Spanish. Nuyorican. That's all any Puerto Rican in New York spoke. A lot of them could only understand Spanish when their mothers yelled at them. I understood the important things: "What'd you say about my girlfriend?" I could ask. Or: "Hey, don't call me a faggot!" If you respond with one of those two, the odds are pretty good that it'll be the right comeback.

There are ten ways to accuse someone of being gay in Puerto Rican Spanish. They may be homophobic, and yet they make the most beautiful transgender women this side of Malaysia.

Puerto Rican life is an all-ages show—teenagers, grandparents, babies, all together, eating stew off of paper plates. No one's too young or too old for any party. They're multigenerational and love children. They will point to a woman's son and say, "He needs a sister. Where's his sister?"

Puerto Ricans are always partying. They're always welcoming you into a loud, noisy apartment. *Vamos. Que quieres para beber?* What you want to drink? *Cambiar el pañal del bebé.* Change the baby's diaper. *Mantenga la puerta abierta.* Leave the door open.

One group of Puerto Ricans on my corner was a biker gang called the 69ers. They had the jackets, the tattoos, the chains. There was only one problem—no motorcycles. Maybe they were making a statement about identity and the arbitrary way we define ourselves—challenging our narrow concepts about what membership in a certain club entails.

There were some white gangs, named by street. The black kids more or less subscribed to the Articles of Confederation. They were a loosely aligned group of states that came together when it was mutually beneficial but otherwise were sovereign according to housing complex. But the Puerto Ricans really took gangs to another level. They had medieval names, like the Savage Nomads, Savage Lords, and Savage Skulls. (There were fewer intellectual property laws around back then.)

One day, I was standing on the Coney Island boardwalk when fifty members of the Puerto Rican gang the Crazy Homicides came running right at me screaming. I stood there facing sure death. Then they ran by me like I was invisible, because it turned out they were just chasing some other gang in patched cut-off jean jackets.

The Puerto Ricans were always on the corner. They were out there, talking to everyone, never finishing a sentence without stretching out the words because they talk so fast. They are always moving furniture. They would say hello by saying, "Yo, grab the other end of this couch." There's always a flurry of activity and they're always around each other. You'd never just see one Puerto Rican.

Puerto Ricans never go inside. Even when they're inside, they're outside: leaning out the window, setting up chairs on the sidewalk, or watching TV on the fire escape with a cord down to the streetlight. The ironing board is the card table. The mailbox is a chair. Someone's cooking on the stoop.

They lean in every car that comes up the block. There's music blasting, the doors are open. It's a carnival atmosphere. People are always eating things off sticks—ices or corn or mangoes or chicken. There's always dominoes, kids with yo-yos and handballs. They will make a party wherever they are, at any time of the day or night.

I went to Puerto Rico once. By the hotel there was a cockfighting ring the size of a small theater—not Madison Square Garden big, but big like a place where you might see a band that was hot ten years ago. Only, in the center were a couple of Cornish hens wearing box cutters taped to their claws.

The Puerto Rican Day parade sums it all up. It's sort of like the St. Patrick's Day parade, only with movement below the waist. And instead of getting knocked out by a three-hundred-pound redheaded electrician's apprentice because you sat on his Jets jacket, you get to watch as three hundred flag-wearing teenagers coming from court appearances cheer on a parade of girls in confirmation dresses riding atop papier-mâché-covered floats resting on stolen cars. The parade ends at a chop shop. And then there is a barbecue.

* * *

Some guys loved black girls and some guys loved white girls, but everybody loved the Puerto Rican girls. They just knew they had it going on—earrings, bracelets, tube tops and the accent. That's what really got everybody. They would answer in class in that Spanish accent and every guy in there would swoon.

Any time Puerto Rican guys had sex, it was out of their control. They would always blame the girl: "She was all over me! The minute I shut the door! I was like, '*Oye*, you sure you wanna do this? You got a boyfriend!'" As if they were innocents being ravaged.

I had no shot at that age. Once again, my game was pretty weak. I know this because once, when I was eleven, a girl invited me to "watch TV" up at her apartment, and when we got up there her mom wasn't home and the TV was in the bedroom, and I lay on the bed with her and watched an entire episode of *Dark Shadows*. I lay on the bed as stiff as an Olympic luger without making a move. I can still see the disgust on her face when we left. Her nickname was "Alleycat" for chrissakes. I don't care how young you are: If you can't make a move on a girl who calls herself Alleycat, you deserve to be chemically castrated.

Which is not to say I was totally sexless when I was young. In elementary school, I had a hot and tawdry encounter with a girl from my block, Angela. Amazing, isn't it, how you don't remember the name of the teacher who taught you how to read, but the name of the girl who let me pull down her underwear in my backyard I'll probably yell in my death throes as I lie on my co-paid mattress in a nursing home, staring out the window at a billboard advertising the one millionth episode of *Comedy Central Presents*.

I even remember everything about Angela's house and her mother, who wore a kerchief over her hair, cat's-eye glasses, and Capri pants with cameltoe. In the early sixties, it was actually all the rage to rock a pair of stretch pants and to sport your cameltoe almost like a family crest. Perhaps it was a precursor to the braless days of the women's liberation movement, which was then still a few years away.

Angela's mother told us to call her "Candy." It was confusing. We were raised to call adults "Mrs." or "Mr." We were not ready for that kind of informality, especially since she wasn't even fat and didn't seem like she was going to tell us the story behind how she acquired such a curious nickname.

That afternoon with Angela was just one of those spontaneous acts of passion that happen between two young people who never thought of each other in sexual terms except for that one afternoon. I remember that childhood indiscretion with Angela fondly—it was my first sexual experience and my first cockblock (my mother broke it up after twenty seconds). If I'd been aware of how long I'd have to wait after that to actually have sex, I can assure you she would've gotten more than just my alarmingly feminine little-boy mitts. But I guess it's Monday morning quarterbacking best left for the imaginations of future guests of Chris Hansen.

I am going to tell you another story. Some of you will think this one is child abuse, but of the five children present, I doubt one could look you in the eyes and say it was destructive to them in any way. I find it sad when you have these boys nailing their female teachers and there's hand-wringing, head-shaking, and cries of "There's a double standard when it comes to female teachers and male teachers charged with sex abuse!"

Yeah, I wonder why. Because it's different! Why? Don't ask me why. You just know! Because the boys in most of these cases say they didn't feel intimidated, or tricked, or taken advantage of, and because it's a lot harder for a woman to physically rape a man.

I would love to interview some of these "victims" and see how they've progressed in the years since they were "brutally ravaged." They're probably like most rape victims: suicidal, depressed, and living in fear. Oh no? You mean they are cocky dudes that parade around town pointing at people and smiling when strangers yell out "You the man"?

When I was about ten years old, my friends and I were invited to stay overnight at the home of these two brothers who we had started to hang out with. Now, their father was a divorced, hip, good-looking dude. And the first time we slept over, he took us all to have a cookout in Prospect Park. So it's about five of us kids plus the father and his hot, voluptuous blonde hippie girlfriend.

We're sitting there—hot dogs, marshmallows, bullshit, bullshit. And then I forget how the subject got introduced, but suddenly we had the shirt and pants of this Nordic Midwestern bombshell half off and we were groping her like an X-rated *Snow White and the Seven Dwarfs*. Like a porno *Gulliver's Travels*—little Lilliputians in the moonlight crawling over her creamy body. Like a Bosch painting of a *Partridge Family* after-party.

If you think I'm imagining this, I'm not. I recently spoke to a friend who was there and he brought it up. Can you imagine being that age and having this swinging-seventies hottie being selfless enough to offer up her body to the greater cause of boyhood developmental pleasure? She'd be in prison for doing that today, but we all know it's a victimless crime.

This same generous divorced dad lived in Crown Heights on the other side of the park. So we went to stay over another night. This time he's got a beautiful little big-eyed brunette there, the kind who in a Paris café you'd find arguing and chain-smoking, throwing up her hands in futility while trying to convince you that *Candide* is hopelessly patriarchal. Then she slumps down in her chair, pouts, and pulls the strings on her Che Guevara hoodie and stares moodily out the window at the Algerian kicking wife number eleven down the Champs-Élysées.

In any case, I somehow found myself sitting in the bedroom with the dad and his *gamine* girlfriend. I managed to make it known that I was down for a replay of the Prospect Park picnic. Well, this dude looks at his girlfriend the way players everywhere have for millennia, with that look like, "Babe?" And this young lady, like the smitten, unquestioning girlfriends of this type of dude everywhere, throughout history, lifted her shirt and gave me a look at her small but truly incredible, looks-good-under-a-poncho-at-a-Jackson-Browne-concert titties.

Unfortunately, I was already a little bit of a compulsive, and I wore out my welcome after the third or fourth flash request. I don't know if I was expecting to be invited to a little bit of the old ménage, or double-duty action, but wherever it was I wanted things to go, they didn't go there, and the dad kicked me out of the bedroom. Apparently the charity of free love and flower power was overcome that night by the dark forces and single-minded neurological depravity of Irish Catholicism. Oh well. Their loss.

* * *

Within an umbrella term like "Hispanic" there are always going to be rivalries and hierarchies. You had to remember the rules: Don't call a Colombian a Cuban. Don't call a Cuban a Puerto Rican. Don't call a Puerto Rican a Dominican. Don't call a Dominican a Mexican. And don't call anybody a Salvadoran.

The Dominicans—or *Domos*, as they don't like to be called—are too Puerto Rican for the Puerto Ricans. They talk faster and louder. They dance more. They play music at a higher volume. They lean out the windows farther. And they are somehow even more emotional.

We did *Oklahoma!* in junior high school, and the lead was Dominican, likely the first Dominican in the U.S. It was an all-star cast: Orlando, who years later got down in front of me and knocked out 653 push-ups in a row; Dartagnan, the world's largest Puerto Rican; Carlos Jesse, who was black and became a very successful preacher in NYC; and finally, yours truly, CQ. I was white but playing it Iranian.

The girls were: Judy, who was Irish, who ran out of class crying because the teacher was discussing Vietnam and her brother was over there; Greta, who was Jewish and from my block and so beautiful. I saw her recently and I almost said, "You look the same as you did in *Oklahoma!*" but I realized that would be creepy because she'd been thirteen, so I stopped myself.

Right, so Orlando with all those push-ups: The Dominicans take over in every situation. They kiss everybody when they enter a room. They fight, they play baseball, and they work for Time Warner Cable.

* * *

One of the largest Latino groups in New York today is Mexicans. Mexican immigrants work at my gym, cleaning. They watch all these people climbing fake walls, rowing fake rowboats, running on fake ground. Meanwhile, to get over here they had to climb real hills, row in real water, run over real highways. It's like all our ancestors came over here and busted their asses building railroads and tunnels and bridges so the kids could have a better life and make good money. Then we spend the money going to the gym to try to look like we still build bridges and tunnels and railroads.

Things Mexicans are single-handedly keeping alive in this nation: boxing, repair work, and the Catholic Church.

Mexican boxers never quit in a fight. You have to knock them out. There are no white towels in Mexican boxing. It's a matter of national pride.

At my gym, you can see the look of frustration on the Mexican workers' faces as one of the trainers teaches a boxing class. The trainer is not a boxer. And yet every Mexican kid has at least one junior welterweight belt sitting on the mantel next to his picture of the Sacred Heart. They put the boys in the ring at three. While other kids are still drawing with crayons, these kids are learning how to wrap their hands. Their father is setting up playdates with Freddie Roach. When these kids get a time out, it's a standing eight count. Other parents are looking for a safe private school. These kids' parents want to find a good cutman.

It's a Hispanic thing, the love of boxing. This Puerto Rican kid on my block growing up, Manuel, got it into his head one day that I was strong for my size, and that of course meant that I must be destined to be a great fighter. Like some kind of miniature Latino Don King, he took me down to the Puerto Rican block to introduce me around and have me fight this tough kid. I was maybe eight.

"Yeah!" I thought. "I guess I am a great fighter!" I was totally into it—until the fight started, at which point I realized I was totally overmatched. Halfway through the fight, Manuel realized it, too, and so he called it off and took me back home. We walked home silently together. "I thought this kid was something," he was muttering.

I worked with a couple of Mexican guys in restaurants,

and they could fix anything. They would just stare at whatever it was—a broken stove or an electrical problem—for ten minutes and then grab a kitchen knife and a piece of gum and it would be fixed. And then they'd jump on the bike and make a delivery in 5-degree weather.

One time when I was a dishwasher, I was working with this Mexican guy—just me and him downstairs—and a giant rat appears on top of the sink where we are washing dishes. Looking right at us with a mean look. I froze and was about to start screaming like a girl in a horror movie. The guy with me doesn't flinch. He picks up a frying pan, beats it to death, and puts it in the garbage. Then he smiles at me, and says "Rata" and nods respectfully like *that was a big one*. And this kid was probably all of sixteen years old and maybe weighed 120 pounds.

Mexicans were meant to be on the West Coast. They've got that slow, laid-back mentality. Even the gang members have that scary affectlessness: "I'm furious, holmes. I'm gonna kill somebody." And all the while their face is a total blank.

Like the Irish, they have drinking issues, to put it mildly. They love drinking. It might be the Indian blood. Because they can do that blank-face thing, they always manage to make it to the bar and act sober enough to order.

Mexicans love death. They like skulls. Skull candy. Skeleton figures. Skull decorations. Maybe it's because skulls are stripped down, like their cars? That's why they like Morrissey. He can sell out Mexico City. I think it's because the nation's identity is half goth morbidity and half grunge sincerity.

The homes of the Mexicans I have known have always been surrounded by a chain-link fence and packed with tools. If I ever wanted to borrow a tool, that's where I would find it. Armed with only a hammer and a box of nails, Mexican workers can build you a house for under a thousand dollars. And it will be a nice house.

They talk about cars the way Shakespeare spoke of love.

> *The timing gears worn you got a faulty fan clutch*
> *cooling fan motor water pump radiator fan*
> *motor power steering pump. Brake drum.*
> *Clutch master cylinder. Differential rear axle.*
> *Pinion seal. Tail pipes. All out of joint.*
> *O cursed spite that I was born to set it right.*

* * *

Hispanics are every shade of black, white, and brown, with every kind of hair—kinky, straight, and stars buzzed into their sideburns. Puerto Ricans were the go-between for black and white. When the Puerto Ricans were around, they kind of brought a sanity to racial tension and today they basically act as the translators for all the various Latino groups. Blessed are the peacemakers, because they will be called children of God, or in this case the children, cousins, aunts, godparents, and the guy down the block who got roped into carrying a chair down the stairs.

IV

Smoked Salmon Pink

I'M CAUTIOUS WITH THIS SECTION, BECAUSE I KNOW THAT JEWS are the only ones who are actually going to read this book. Lenny Bruce always said everybody from New York is Jewish, whether they're Jewish or not, and nobody from outside New York can be Jewish, even if they are. As Jews, they spread out to the suburbs, except Long Island, and they became less and less Jewish. The Jews in Beverly Hills are less Jewish than I am. I'm not saying Jews from Chicago can't be funny, but name some. Canadians can't be Jews, so they don't count.

If you are driving to a synagogue that's on a beautiful manicured lawn, you no longer have a Jewish vibe. A synagogue should be on a dirty street and you congregate afterward and argue about who's taking the train back to the other borough and who can drive who and who wants to stay and go get something to eat and he can't take the bus what are you crazy he's senile your gonna put him on the bus? They were made to take the subway and live in apartments. Once they move to a house, they're not as funny. A house isn't funny. A car isn't funny. A tenement is funny. The train is funny. Aggravation is funny. Jews in the suburbs have to manufacture aggravation.

The Brooklyn Jews for the most part did not have money. They lived in apartments in Brighton Beach and Coney Island before it became Little Odessa. They lived in Flatbush by Ocean Parkway, but that was it for the regular Jews...by which I mean the non-Hasidic ones. Hasids are the hard-core special forces of Jews. They were showing out every day in Williamsburg and Crown Heights when those were damn rough neighborhoods. They were rocking those hats and coats and payos and strutting down Eastern Parkway and going "Yeah, we're the Jews, so what's up?" It's the same with Muslim jihadists. Even though you don't think they represent your religion well, it's hard not to feel like a half stepper when they're willing to die for the Book and you haven't even been to Mecca because you're waiting until you get enough Delta miles to fly business class.

They always want to know the details, the Jews. They want to know the *mechanisms*. My friend Lauren was crying one day when I met her for lunch, and I said, "What's wrong?" She proceeded to tell me how her mother and aunt verbally excoriated her for paying too many points on the closing costs for her new apartment. They do a thorough investigation and spend the next few months talking about fair market value adjustable rate mortgage refinance sweat equity. Meanwhile, any other culture, somebody gets a new apartment and everybody just goes "Wow, that sounds cool. Where is it?" Not the Jews. They are living in the real world. They want the specifics.

And they want to know who's in charge of everything. Okay, so who's the company president? Okay, is he the final word, or is there a board he has to answer to? One Jewish comic I know called me and asked me where I was performing in Philadelphia. "The Suzanne Roberts Theatre, huh?" he asked me. "Who's this Suzanne Roberts that she has her own theater?" I could hear him googling her in the background.

The Jews can never stop themselves from saying something. They always have to have the last word. The worst thing you can say to them is, "I don't want to talk about it!" That's where you lose the Jews. They want to talk about it all. Why wouldn't you want to talk about it?

Jews ask fifty questions until they feel confident that they have a sense of how everything is going. At a restaurant, they lean over and ask, "What are you eating? Do you like it?" Even in their religious ceremonies, *why is this day different from any other day?* What did you pay? And if you are a goy you answer, "I'm not sure." They'll say, "How could you not be sure? You're throwing your money away!!" That's a very big insult coming from a Jew. They're in your business—right *there*. They're the only ones who care. Then they sum it up in a business-minded way: "Okay. So you're working on this book." And then the conversation can move on.

The Jews like to talk it through. They don't like to stuff down their thoughts. They don't internalize and yet they still all have digestive problems. Their minds are always racing. They're walking around in different stages of physical discomfort real and imagined at all times. Between the real problems (the allergies, sinuses, many foot problems) and the issues that are psychosomatic but no less painful, as any true Jew will remind you (such as stomach pain, anxiety, back pain, neck pain), these are people who are living and working next to you while thinking about how long the line at Walgreens will be if they go during lunch. Is it genetic, a physical startle response based on the pogroms and invasions of their history? Is that why at least one child in the family is encouraged to become a doctor?

Jews only listen to other Jews anyway, so this is falling on deaf ears, I realize that. If you give your opinion on a movie or restaurant or anything to a Jewish friend, they look at you politely and go "Oh really? Interesting." But they've already discounted what you said. If another Jewish person says the same place is good, then they make a reservation. Their big word with each other is "recommendation." Do you *recommend* we go see that show? You say it was a good resort but would you *recommend* it? Do you like the 228? The Gran Coupe? Would it be something you'd recommend or...?

Jews do know quality, you can't deny it. My mother said the reason we had a nice house growing up was because her friend Naomi would always gently steer her away from the cheesy rug or the ugly curtains and say, "You know, this one is almost the same price and it's actually kind of a stronger material." And that's the thing. People say Jews are cheap but really they'll just pay the value of what something's worth, and they're not afraid to talk about money. Everybody else is either ashamed to talk money or just starts to get crazy. Jews talk about money like it's a subject worth discussing, which it is.

That's one of the things that separate the Jews: They don't get tired during negotiations; they get energized. They like to explore the fine print, and if your eyes glaze over and you settle without doing your due diligence, well, next time hire a Jew to look it over for you.

Not that there aren't Jews that are chiselers. When they're like that, there's nobody more brutal. It's not pretty when you find yourself in "negotiations" with a garmento who's trying to get rid of a container of last year's Jessica Simpson handbags.

Or if you live in New York, all the moving services are Israeli. And you should see them. Rude. Pushing your couch down the stairs. Throwing your pets out the window. If that's how they moved the Palestinians, no wonder there's riots. With even a simple apartment move you've got the Bar-Lev brothers moving my sectional to the '67 borders.

Yes, Israelis are another type of Jew entirely. They look like Arabs, they act like Italians, but they have last names like the prescriptions list at the Jericho LensCrafters. They're always rushing you, whether you're telling a story and they want to hear the end or it's time for dinner and they want you to come sit down at the table already. *They're* not in a rush. They put *you* in a rush. They speak in a clipped way, as if you're the slowest person in the world.

Then there's the Russian Jews. They came in as Jews seeking asylum and somehow they transformed into the bad guys in every TV show or movie. They're the politically correct villains. In real life they all live in Brighton Beach and Miami, anywhere there's an ocean. They always live near the ocean so they must love it, but you would never know because they don't smile. The Russian Jews are so pushy and annoying that they drive the Israelis crazy. And the Israelis drive the Hasidic Jews crazy. And the Hasids drive the Orthodox crazy. And they all drive the American Jews crazy.

Jews love culture. They read, they love the theater, the museums, Lincoln Center. And they support those places. Without them the whole country would be like Branson, Missouri. Go to a cultural center anywhere in the country, no matter where, and even if there are no Jews it's the Maurice and Florence Rosenthal Center for Art of Wyoming, the Herman and Lillian Tannenbaum Historical Museum of

NASCAR of Rural Arkansas. They love a plaque. If Jews have plaques they can die happy.

The Jews are known for their sense of humor, as they often remind us. The Jews are the only ones that make street jokes about themselves: Two garment-center *machers* meet in Miami during fashion season, when theoretically they should be working in New York rather than laying out on the beach. One says, "Sol, what are you doing here? It's the middle of the season."

"We had a fire," Sol says.

Murray nods in understanding.

Then Sol says, "For that matter, Murray, what are *you* doing here?"

Murray says, "We had a flood."

Sol says, "How do you make a flood?"

Not that other races didn't do such things throughout New York's history (see *Goodfellas*), but the burning of the Bronx in the 1970s, which involved Puerto Ricans with gas cans hired by businessmen to turn Southern Boulevard into the South Dakota prairie, was not for nothing known as "Jewish lightning." People in any group will abuse the honor system, but it's the way in which you rob that makes each race unique. Jews did it through the system. Italians did it through the unions. Blacks did it through the roof. But it all had the same result.

In the 1980s, there were "Polo crews" in New York City who would steal the hell out of Ralph Lauren clothes from stores. Picture Ralph Lauren, the former Ralph Lifshitz of the Bronx, sipping a cocktail in the Hamptons and then getting a call about a major Polo crew theft. The shock sends him back to his garmento roots, and he's yelling into the phone, *"The schvartzers are robbing me blind."*

* * *

I was twenty-five the first time I saw the Comedy Cellar. Manny Dworman, who ran the place, was from Tel Aviv. Estee Adoran, the booker, who'd fought in the Israeli army, was the only person in New York who smoked more than I did. Manny loved telling Jewish jokes. A waitress would come up to say something to him while he was talking to a group of Hasidim and he'd say, loudly, "Wait! Don't talk about money around the Jews."

One of his favorite Jewish jokes:

A Jew is on his deathbed. "Where are my children?" he calls. "Where is my eldest, David?"

"I'm here, Papa," says David.

"Where is my daughter? Where's Sarah?"

"I'm here, Papa," says Sarah.

"And Seth? Where's my Seth?"

"I'm here," says Seth. "We're all here, Papa."

"Then who," the old man says, "is watching the store?"

When I started in stand-up comedy, it was mostly Jews. They were the ones that started the business, I think in the vaudeville days. Because to be a comedian, believe it or not, you have to be intelligent. Most Jews are pretty smart. But the dumb ones become businessmen. The smart ones become doctors or lawyers or teachers or writers, and the dummies go into business. It's always been that way. That's part of what makes America amazing and annoying: You can be a fuckin' idiot and still get rich.

The Jews invented the comedy scene, and when I started, thank God it was Jewish-influenced in New York. Why? Because I had just quit drinking, and after the shows all the Jews would go to the diner. If it had been an Irish scene, it would've been the bar and I would've died in my first year. I guarantee that.

But the Jews were into going to the diner and eating, and that suited me just fine even though I smoked three packs of cigs a day. I would go into that diner with Chris Rock and Adam Sandler and we would write jokes, and I think we all knew even back then that I was going to be the richest and most successful of the three of us.

If it were up to me, I would never let people drink at comedy shows. For some comics it's good having a drunk audience. For me it's bad. I don't want them to "loosen up." I want them to listen to everything I say. That's why I do this for a living: I want people to pay attention to everything that comes out of my mouth.

So you'd go on the road and do these little gigs. New Jersey saved comedy (something I hate to admit). Every night a different bar would have a comedy night, what we called a one-nighter. All the New York City comedians would drive out, three people to a car, and hit these comedy nights in Jersey. That was a show.

We performed sometimes in a place where the Irish still held sway—the Boston scene. The first time I went up there, in the mid-eighties, I met the big four icons of Boston comedy: Steve Sweeney, Lenny Clarke, Kenny Rogerson, and Don Gavin. They were all brilliant, all hilarious. Back then Pablo Escobar had them on speed dial.

They'd bring liquor onstage. If they could have found a way to bring coke on, they would have. They said, "Make sure you mention all my credits in my intro," so they'd have time to do that extra line before they went on.

They were so funny. But it was hard for them. Jerry Seinfeld said it best: "The best part of your day—the part when you're the happiest and highest—has to be stand-up. Otherwise you're not going to want to do it. You have to be miserable in the rest of your life, or else you're not going to want to go up there."

* * *

Now let's talk about the vicious, mean-spirited, and completely accurate stereotype that the Jews run show business. Gary Oldman came out in a *Playboy* interview saying some things to that effect. In his profuse apology, written more or less in Yiddish, you will note he didn't say that Jews *don't* run Hollywood.

Mel Gibson was the biggest name in Hollywood. Movie star and director. He pissed off the tribe with *The Passion of the Christ* and then he made some anti-Semitic remarks, and now he's sharing a trailer with Ronda Rousey on the set of *The Expendables 4*. And why? Because he's anti-Semitic? So what? If you kill a guy like that over a couple of anti-Semitic remarks, you reinforce all the beliefs that the Jews control the business and will take you down if you mess with them. I mean, even if it's true, you don't want to make it that obvious.

"The Jews." You even say "the Jews" and everybody starts to tighten up. A lot of people are still anti-Semitic. They attach mysterious properties to the Jews because they've been so successful. People are pissed off and jealous. But nobody ever asks how do they do it. Luckily, I've figured it out.

People say Jews are pushy. They are! They get in your face. That's how they get things, like Hollywood. They understand how the system is set up. To get anywhere you have to incessantly ask for explanations. Once you do that, you have power. People want you out of their face.

Let's say you're Irish and you hear about a job through a friend of the family. This friend tells your mother to tell you to call up the guy. You call up. The guy tells you there's no job. You tell your mother. She says, "That's bullshit. Why would our friend tell us there's a job when there's no job? I knew he was a phony. He's always been like that." Never talks to the guy again. Every time that guy's name comes up, your family tells the story of the time he said there was a job and you called and looked like a fool. You all take it personally. Very personally. It was humiliating.

The Jews don't take it personally. Same scenario. You hang up. There's no job. The mother questions you as to what was said, what questions he asked, etc. You don't give satisfactory answers. Your mother calls. "Hi, my son called on the recommendation of a mutual friend and now he's telling me there's no job. I'm just curious as to why we're having a miscommunication?" The guy is cold. The Jews don't like the cold. She calls up the original friend and says, "We called and something very strange happened. This guy was less than forthcoming. We weren't pushing him. If there's no job there's no job, but I was just trying to clarify, and he was not rude but maybe...preoccupied? Should we just forget it or..." The mutual friend says, "What? Forget it!? No, he told me there was a job. Let me call him!" He calls the guy but the guy says he'll have to get back to him. Now the whole community is in an uproar. People are giving the job guy side glances at temple. People are wondering, "What's the kid supposed to do? Everybody needs a job! What if his kid needs a job someday and somebody does that to him? How would he like it?" Finally the guy gives up and says, "Okay! I'm sorry! I didn't think his voice was right. It's a customer service job!" And people say, "Well, okay, just say so. If he's not right for the job, he's not right for the job. Not all jobs fit all people. Is there anything else coming up that he might be more suited for? Doesn't hurt to ask, right?"

Jews know that you don't have to pay off a boss when you can harass them for weeks on end. They know that most bosses hire people they know, or people they want to get out of their face. You might be more likely to hire the girl one of your aunts in the Five Towns keeps calling you about, saying, "She's out there in L.A.! Can't you at least get her a meeting?" Or the guy your uncle points to at synagogue and says, "Look, he's here every week! He's a nice kid. There's nothing for him?"

* * *

When MTV launched the game show *Remote Control* in 1987, Ken Ober was the host and I was the announcer. The concept was that Ken was hosting the show in his basement, and sometimes "Ken's mother" would yell at him from off-screen. The way the game worked, there were three contestants seated in recliners, answering trivia questions. Some of the questions were acted out in skits. There were snack breaks, where the contestants would have food dropped on them. And the recliners would go back through the wall. This was considered pretty wild at the time. Everybody loved it but me. I was the comedy snob.

Ken Ober, who was an anti-Semitic Jew, was always taunting his Jewish manager, who with his two other powerful, very show-business friends played so strongly into stereotypes: "The three of you sitting in a diner, sending back your food five times, talking to the waitress for an hour about your low-salt diets and then leaving a terrible tip are why there were pogroms in Russia."

But Ken was a party guy, and he loved being on TV. We'd go to all these parties together—MTV producers, cast, writers, crew, everybody. The forty of us would run around New York and dance at clubs until all hours. Still, I kept feeling like our talents were being wasted. After one live show, I was complaining to Ken about how we should be working on our stand-up rather than doing this bullshit, and what about our integrity as comedians?

A hot girl walked up to us with a Sharpie, pulled her shirt down, and said, "Will you sign my tits?"

While I was signing, Ken turned to me and said, "What were you saying, *Spalding Gray*?"

The effect that show had on girls was too much power for any one man, really. Once when we were shooting in Florida for Daytona Beach Spring Break 1989 we went to a strip club and all the strippers left their customers-with-money to come hang out with us.

One night, I was in an elevator with the comedian Sam Kinison and his entourage and a bunch of strippers from the club. They had a ridiculously giant plastic container full of coke. It looked like a prop from the set of *Scarface*. They were going back to Sam's hotel room for an insane coke-fueled orgy.

I'd quit drinking by this point, and usually I could hang out, but sometimes I just had to go home.

Sam and Ken and all the strippers had assumed I was going with him. Because who wouldn't? We'd all been laughing for an hour beforehand. But I knew I couldn't go to that room or it would be all over for me. I might make it through that night, but I'd be dead within a week. I hit the button for the twelfth floor, where my room was. The doors opened and I stepped off the elevator.

"Good night," I said.

"You're not coming up?" Sam asked, baffled. "You should come up!"

I shook my head.

They were all struck dumb—all these strippers, bouncers, Sam, Kenny. The last thing I saw before the elevator doors closed was all of them standing there silently staring at me, their brows furrowed.

"How was it?" I asked Sam the day after his hotel-room gathering.

"Exactly what it should have been," Sam said. And that was somehow worse than getting all the details.

* * *

When I was on MTV, I had a little heat. Casting agents would bring me to Hollywood for meetings to talk about projects. "You'll be reading for the producers," my agent would tell me.

I'd walk into the room and sit down, cross my legs, light up a cigarette, and start talking with usually about five assembled producers, big network people. Before we did the read-through, they would almost always say, "So what did you think of the script?" And I would almost always say, "It's shit, but me and my friends could rewrite it for you."

I figured these suits would appreciate my honesty, and my ambition, and how willing I was to bail out whoever the schmuck was they had writing these rough drafts for them.

I'd feel a little tension in the room, but I assumed that was just because they weren't used to that kind of New York realness. I'd read a bit and then I'd leave, and later I'd call my agent.

"How'd I do?" I'd ask.

"They hate you!" my agent would say. "I don't know what you did, but whatever it was, they *hated* it."

This same scenario repeated several times. I never got a sitcom, and my career never went to the places some of my friends' careers went. And I always wondered why. My agent and I never put two and two together.

Then, years later, I was talking with some friends of mine in the business, and based on what they were saying, I realized with a horror-movie "The call is coming from inside the house": *The writers are the producers.* The producers are the writers. All over Hollywood, for years, I had systematically gone around telling all the most powerful sitcom writers—*to their faces*—that they were horrible writers and I could do better. So my sitcom never happened. The only way I console myself is I think that if I had ended up doing those shows, I probably would've had a brick drop on my head on the set and died. That's how I comfort myself when I miss great shots: I might've ended up getting in some random accident that killed me. Thank God I didn't get the gig.

* * *

I've always believed that my relentlessness was a sign that I am secretly Jewish. You can't tell me "no" without giving me a reason, and if you try to kick me out of some place, I won't leave without making a scene. And so I clung to show business. In 1988, I wound up with a line in the movie *Crocodile Dundee II*. That was a big deal at the time for a comedian—to have an actual line in an actual movie—and the first *Crocodile Dundee* had been a phenomenon, so I knew that, especially with me in it, this one would be even bigger.

Then I read the script. I was disappointed. In the first part of the film, a drug lord kidnaps Dundee's girlfriend and he has to run around New York trying to save her.

"This isn't New York the way it really is!" I said. And then I made the leap that had stood me in such good stead up to that point: "What this script needs is a complete rewrite."

My problem is I never look at anyone as my superior. I looked on them as my equals. I fervently believed that there were only about ten movies in the history of the cinema that couldn't have benefited from a rewrite by me: the first two *Godfather* movies, *Taxi Driver*, *Goodfellas*, a couple others.

Everything else: "You know what this needs? A couple of scenes written by me."

Well, *Crocodile Dundee II* needed more than just a couple of scenes. For starters, something had to be done about how fake the New York City stuff was. Luckily, I could help them there. Who knew New York better than I did? No one. I got right to work, redoing the whole thing. My poor girlfriend Lia typed it up for me—this was back in the typewriter days. There I was, feverishly writing, handing her pages, crossing things out, going full newsroom-city-desk. She was sitting there and thinking, "What a delusional fuckin' loser I've got for a boyfriend."

In the real script—or what I began to refer to as "the first draft"—a character named Leroy Brown, played by the actor Charles S. Dutton, led Paul Hogan around New York. In my version—which I called "the second draft"—Charles Dutton was out and now Paul Hogan's character was being led around New York by a real, streetwise New Yorker, "Kevin Murphy," played by—who else?—me. (Murphy is my mother's maiden name.)

I'd like to point out now that anybody can get it into his head to rewrite a script and to fantasize about fighting his way out of the chorus into a leading role. Any deluded ass-hole can do that. But you have to be a true psychotic to hand it in. I handed it in. I waited to hear the response, which never came. If only they'd let me replace Charles Dutton in that film, I bet it would have made a lot more than the paltry $240 million it took in worldwide. I met Charles Dutton once, and I wondered if he—an ex-boxer, by the way—ever suspected that I tried to rob him of his big movie role.

* * *

When I got to *Saturday Night Live*, everyone was saying it was about to go under. That year I became a featured player, 1995–96, was supposed to be the repair year. There were a whole new bunch of people there like Will Ferrell and Cheri Oteri, who were the early ones who saved the show, along with Lorne Michaels.

I started out on the show as a writer. We were snobs in that writers' room—which, by the way, had almost no Jews in it. *Saturday Night Live* has always had a weirdly low percentage of Jews for show business—the lowest, I'd wager, of any show that ever lasted more than a year.

When I started out, there was only one Jewish writer at *SNL*. Everyone else was Irish and Italian. The Jewish guy would say, "We have to do it eventually, right? Let's just get it done."

The rest of us were always like, "Hold on a second! I just want to say one thing before we start. First of all, who's this fucking Lorne telling me what to do? Fuck him! Fuck them!" Then we would do it. Germanic people, Jews, and Chinese people want to finish something. The rest of us feel that it's important to do a certain amount of protesting first.

Lorne would come in and say, "Do Cheerleaders again!" And we would all groan and roll our eyes. That skit of Will Ferrell and Cheri Oteri's, where they play wannabe

Spartans cheerleaders, was funny the first time, but again? But Lorne knew: Especially with people watching the show less and less, it was important to give viewers something to grasp on to.

The most beautiful thing about *Saturday Night Live* was the Wednesday read-through. That was where, if you were a writer or performer on that show, you could try out anything in front of an audience of about a hundred people, including everyone from that week's host and your fellow cast members to the makeup and crew people and the art department. It would be like, "For the next five minutes, you people are going to see what I got." And Lorne would be like, "Whadda you got? Let's hear it. If you got something, people will know." And they would. They'd seen everything and were ready to laugh, but had no reason to if you weren't funny.

On every other show, you'd show your pages to your friends on the show and they'd say, "It's great! Go with that!" Every time you're in a movie, at the screening everyone tells you it's brilliant, you're brilliant, and it's going to be a monster hit. But on *SNL*, there was a truly neutral audience, and the read-through was an actual test. That's as fair a shot as you can get on this earth.

That's why that show lasts, all because of Lorne sitting there on Wednesdays saying to these people he's hired, "You're telling me you're funny. Here's your moment every week." If there's silence at the end of that five minutes, he doesn't have to say anything.

Could Lorne turn cold on you sometimes? Yes. Would he roll his eyes at some of your skits? Sure. (I hear now he's looking at his phone. At least he's doing something other than staring at the ceiling while he's killing your stuff.) But also, imagine the show that he created from his point of view, watching all these innocent people come in and get successful and start to change. That can be annoying, I'm sure.

You have to value what you do if you want everyone else to. I learned that once when I did a show in New Jersey with no cover charge. I had this delusion that the crowd was going to be great, because they'd be psyched to be getting something for free. No, they were the worst. As a rule, the more an audience has to pay, the better a crowd they are. People don't appreciate something that comes for free, so you have to feel confident enough to demand what you're worth.

The people who rise to the top in show business have that killer instinct. They don't like to admit it. They're all talented, but they also have something else, and I'm not sure what the word is, but I know it's not compassion. They say, "I'm not going to kick you off the ladder, but just so you know, I'm going up first." I don't know where I got it. My family is all teachers. I'm the only one swaggering around like this.

You know what I hate? The people who get famous and then get humble. You see them accepting awards and saying, "I'm amazed! I can't believe I'm around all these famous people! I can't believe I'm making all this money!" Shut up.

Yes you can. The only way you get there is if you want it and you want it bad. And that Wednesday read-through where all of us could come together and battle it out Thunderdome style? It was a beautiful thing.

* * *

When I was a kid, in between wanting to be black, Italian, Puerto Rican, etc., I felt like a Jew. I would rush home at night when I was ten to watch *Can You Top This?*, a show that featured three comedians that each had to make a contestant laugh or something. I forget the plot. But they'd always have Stu Gilliam, a black comic, Morey Amsterdam, a fat comic, and then Mr. Cool himself—Jan Murray. Who except a ten-year-old future comedian would identify with a dangerously overtanned, blinged-out, chain-smoking, slightly pompous, borscht-belt comic in his late forties? This guy was my idol.

And one of the great moments in my life was when Jerry Seinfeld, who knew about my love for Jan Murray, reached out and got Jan to make a tape for me before he passed away. Of course, he didn't know me from Adam and spent the whole time talking about Jerry and barely mentioned my name, but it didn't matter, because I understood. Why would a Jew waste a tape complimenting a dumb goy that nobody ever heard of when you can make a connection with a big *macher* like Jerry Seinfeld? It was the smart move, Jan. He was still networking even on his deathbed.

Growing up, I knew a lot of Jews without money. Brooklyn was full of tough Jews, real old-school blue-collar fathers who were cabbies or city workers, didn't-move-out-of-East-New-York-till-the-sixties Jews. We kids shared cultures. I taught them how to underage drink and they taught me all about pills. They loved Quaaludes, Tuinals, Nembutals. Even in the drug culture they're still more comfortable when the addictions are related to a physician.

The first time I went to OTB was in the Jewish neighborhood of Luna Park/Trump Village/Warbasse out by Coney Island. If you ever wanted to see racial unity, OTB was the place. You had Jews, Italians, Jamaicans, and Puerto Ricans all unified in their hate of some trainer or some jockey that took the four horse wide. The unifying properties of adrenaline-fueled screaming and praying, followed by the ritual ripping up of tickets and cursing, need to be studied if we are ever to get along. Nobody at OTB was black, white, Spanish, or Asian. They were all just at the mercy of a temperamental thoroughbred, a coked-out trainer, and a hundred-pound Honduran.

Like everybody else, Jews regulate in their own way. When I lived in a predominantly Asian building, and the elevator stopped running, the maintenance guys would make us wait a day or two. They got away with murder because Asians don't complain. But when I lived in a building that was predominantly Jews, if the heat was off for an hour there'd be thirty people in the lobby, muttering to each other, yelling to the skies. They never complained to the staff; they would just complain to each other. "Why is the heat off again?" "This is the third time this month. Is this normal?" "I'm not saying it's your fault but is there a city agency I should call?" "What am I paying rent for?" They're relentless. They don't leave till it's resolved.

I miss the New York Jews. They're not really here anymore. There are people with Jewish last names, but not that old-school personality. Jerry and Neysa Moskowitz, whose daughter Ricki hung out in front of the school with us and whose daughter Stacy was killed by the Son of Sam, went on TV and gave an interview that to this day is one of the saddest and most beautiful—and somehow funniest—interviews epitomizing the Brooklyn Jews of the 1970s. The father, Jerry, was on the street surrounded by other worried people and obviously still in mourning, wearing a white T-shirt if I remember correctly. He started to say what he will do if he ever gets his hands on Son of Sam. And Neysa is next to him and says, "Calm down, Tarzan," half affectionately and half sarcastically.

Most of those Jews are now in West Palm Beach, and the sun doesn't let anyone be themselves. It dries out your real self, and to those aging older people sitting on the bench watching TV and waiting for the end, I say *I remember.* I remember when you set the pace in the city. Cigar chomping, candy store–owning, chowing down on bologna and liverwurst for lunch while arguing over the JDL's right to patrol Wythe Avenue in Williamsburg and then getting on the train back to Co-op City, or Rego Park, or Brightwater

Towers, and waking up the next day groaning and sighing and doing it all again.

Jews are here to remind us that it's okay to ask Why? How much? Who owns this? How come he owns it? How hard could it be? You do the paperwork, you get the loan, you get the license, you get the documentation, you find a manufacturer and a shipping company, and you open up the store, what?

V

Paddy Wagon Green

As far back as I can remember, I always wanted to be a drunken Irish poet. As kids we'd go visit my grandma and grandpa at their bungalow in Breezy Point, Queens—the Irish Riviera. There was a bar right on the beach, and all the adults would sit there and drink and smoke while we played in the sand in front of them. The bar was inside but it had an open front, so you'd be in a dark bar but still on the beach. Because Irish people don't really enjoy the beach. It's probably our number one killer after the booze and the dirty Prods. Irish people can make a pub out of anything. We would come up for a quick soda and we'd smell the cigarettes and beer and see the smiling happy adults, happy because they were falling off their barstools at two o'clock. That Irish cologne of cigarettes, beer, and suntan lotion is in my nostrils today.

Colin Quinn

The bar was a holy place. Now that I think about it, it's probably no accident that the bar and the church both have a similar interior design. Stained glass, dark lighting, dark wood, all the communicants leaning forward and confessing sins and waiting for the bartender's benediction of "Ah, fuck them, you were in the right, I would've done the same thing." I loved bars. Even though I no longer drink and smoke, I still love them. It's not the same, but it's like going to see a really good cover band—it reminds you of how great you were back when Zeppelin were what they were.

Back then, Seventh Avenue had about twenty-five bars lined up from 9th Street to Flatbush. There were the old-man bars, which would only have six customers but the place would never lose money because those guys had pension checks and they'd be waiting outside at 8 a.m. If the bartender was late, he'd get cursed out.

You had the Mafia bar, where every time a stranger came in, the whole bar would go silent—even Sinatra on the jukebox would start singing "Stranger in the Bar." They'd look at your hands, and unless you were dropping off an envelope or a paper bag, you'd better be on your merry way.

Then you had the Irish blackout bars that you would come-to in mid-conversation. Then you had the music bars, where people would pretend to be sophisticated and listen to live music. Then you had the kids' bars, where you could get in even if you were twelve years old as long as you had ID. There were the coke bars where you'd go in, order a drink, take one sip, go to the bathroom, and walk back out. None of the bars served food until 1982. No food, except maybe the old man bar would break out sandwiches to "line the stomach," as the old-timers would say.

There was an old-timers bar on my corner for most of my childhood, called the Stack of Barley. The bartender had a cauliflower nose with varicose veins running through it. That nose probably got more people sober than AA.

I bartended myself back in the day, which was like a wolf guarding the sheep. I was an average bartender, but I worked with a true master named Freddy Cavallero at Knickers on Second Avenue. This guy was good. He would remember everyone's name and everyone's drink. If you came in a year later, he'd remember your first and last name and what you drank. I really felt like he liked me because he knew I worshipped him. Fifteen years later I was on *SNL*; I'm walking out of a trendy pool hall and I see him with his girlfriend. I go, "Freddy, it's me, Colin Quinn!" He looks at me. He's a little tipsy but not that bad. His girlfriend seems to recognize me from comedy or TV. "I used to bartend with you!" I continued. Freddy, the man with the amazing memory, looks at me and says, "I'm supposed to remember every fuckin' guy I bartended with?" And walks away. And that's why he was a great bartender.

* * *

Irish people brought cynicism to New York. All the other immigrants came here brutalized by oppression and corruption, but they all saw that Statue of Liberty. Even the most hardened of them got a little lump in the throat pulling into New York Harbor and seeing Lady Liberty's welcoming gaze. The Irish got here in the 1840s, so there was no Statue of Liberty yet. All we saw was crummy waterfront that looked exactly like the ones we just left.

Members of my family have that wonderfully miserable sense of sarcasm. At my niece's baptism, our "Uncle" Aidan from Ireland was sitting in a nearby pew. When the priest, standing over the baby, asked the godparents, "Do you believe in God, the Father Almighty, Creator of Heaven and Earth?" Aidan yells out from his pew, "No!"

The priest ignored it and continued: "Do you reject Satan and all his works?"

"No!" Aidan yelled again.

What's more cynical than a grown man sitting in a hallowed place on a hallowed occasion inviting the wrath of God, Satan, and all his works onto a newborn baby? But we did all laugh—well, except the priest.

I used to think we were ashamed of emotions in my family. People always say that Irish people aren't "comfortable" with emotions. But that's not it. We're *disgusted* by emotions. We find them ridiculous and phony and embarrassing. You know what annoys Irish people? Enthusiasm. The worst thing you can be around Irish people is overly excited. Do not go up to an Irishman and say, "Hey, dude!" and then start singing "Fairy Tale of New York" by the Pogues. Yes, we sing those songs, and maybe we'll even shed a tear. But only because they're about *other people.*

It's abstract. Only a self-pitying whiner would cry like that for himself.

We don't kiss hello. Italians hug. Jews hug. Our family's Jewish friends would also make little remarks, like, "Oh, look! She's getting *boobies*!" We found that horrifying. Nobody Irish ever goes, "Look how handsome he's getting!" If someone said that to us, we'd go, "What are you, a creep?" Even when Irish people are drinking together and having a blast, they never look like they're having fun. They're not animated. Their shoulders are still rounded even when inside they're full of joy.

Family parties were like a bar in those days. Everybody was smoking and drinking. All the adults would show up with cases of beer and cartons of cigarettes and put their feet up on the table. They'd sing Sinatra and Herb Albert and the Beatles, and you knew it was winding down when my aunt Maureen would start singing in a smoker's voice, "Is That All There Is" by Peggy Lee. "If that's all there is, my friends, then let's keep dancing. Let's break out the booze and have a ball."

* * *

At my father's funeral a couple of years ago, this guy got up and told a story about my father. He told us, "We were getting ready to go to Korea. Your father was a great man. He said to our friend—the retired police captain—'I'm single. You're married. I'll put myself on the list ahead of you.'"

At the wake afterward, somebody brought it up and how amazing it was. And I see my mother sitting there with that look on her face. Like a Nun Sphinx. And I go, "Ma, what's the matter, isn't that an amazing story?"

And she says slowly, "Yeah, do you really think that you get to tell the army that you want to switch places and they say 'Go ahead'? Do you really think that's how things work?"

Not long after that, the police captain slipped on the stairs in his socks. This was a guy who'd been in the army and then served as a police officer during some of the roughest years in New York City. And what gets him? Socks. What a world. That's a typically Irish story—funny but morbid.

Punishment is why we are drawn to law enforcement. It starts early. In an Irish family, the father and mother play "good cop, bad cop" with the kids:

"Son, I heard you quit your job," says the mother.

"Ah, come on, give him a break," says the father.

"I'm not bothering him," says the mother. "Do you feel bothered? Because if you feel bothered, you can quit conversation like you quit your job."

That's the ritual: shame, self-loathing, dark humor, comfort, repeat. The Irish culture is built on shame. If you're late one time, people will bring it up for the rest of your life. Ten years later: "See you there at three—if you're not late again! Like you were that time in 1978."

The Irish were cops back in the day, which makes sense. Even I took the Port Authority police test way out on

Twelfth Avenue. No one walked there at that point unless they were going to take the police test, and when I got there through the empty streets I was surprised to find the test was packed with people. "Wow," I thought, "they need a lot of cops for one bus station." Deluded as I was, I thought the Port Authority police only worked at the Port Authority Bus Terminal. (In fact, they work all the bridges and tunnels and airports.)

I sat for the test and found it incredibly easy. The questions were all like: "Someone comes up to you and says X. Do you (a) Say Y, (b) Get back in the car and drive away, or (c) Run them over." I got a 96 percent.

And yet they never called to offer me a job. I think it's because in those days, before they let you be a cop they went and asked your neighbors about you, and if they did that in my case, they would have gotten some bad reviews (certainly not my last).

It was probably for the best. The only reason I wanted to work at the bus station was because I was going to write a version of Dante's *Inferno* in which the levels of the famously decrepit and sleazy Port Authority Bus Terminal corresponded to the levels of hell. I had it all worked out. Never mind that I hadn't yet read Dante's *Inferno*. I was going to get to that when I got the job—*so it would be fresh in my mind*, I told myself, while I was writing my best-selling book.

At any rate, the Irish were and always will be attracted to the police department, because we believe in punishment.

We believe in atonement. We believe in sin. The Italians and the Puerto Ricans went to church just as much as the Irish but it went in one ear and out the other. They never took it to heart. They'd leave after Mass and they'd be grabbing each other's asses and laughing. The Irish would be walking home and we'd turn to each other: "You know what? That priest made a good point. I really am a sinning piece of shit. God sacrificed His only son for my sins and I still carry on this way? What kind of garbage person would do such a thing?" It just made sense to us. And so it makes sense that so many Irish would become cops.

The Irish set the tone for the police department. Cops are not supposed to physically touch you, so they verbally touch you. They belittle you. "Hey, genius, what does an upside-down triangle mean, hah? Yield. Very good. Yield. You're going to get a gold star! And were you yielding? No. Okay, rocket scientist, this says to appear in court on the sixteenth. Hopefully you can read this, since apparently you couldn't read the yield sign."

Cops have to organize disorganized situations. They're all about placement of people, like street choreographers. "You, with the mouth, you stand over there. Keep your hands where I can see them. You move over next to her. You talk first, then you tell me what happened. Do me a favor, just move back about two feet."

Their job is to use small talk to subtly get you to incriminate yourself. "How you doin' tonight? You doin' good? You guys go out tonight? Have a few drinks? You guys live around here? Where are you coming from? Who's in the backseat?"

This is why shows like *Law & Order* will never really get the cops right—because the shows are too sincere and filled with righteous indignation. I am the only man, woman, or child in the Tri-State area who has never been cast on *Law & Order*. I think it's because no cops on *Law & Order* are Irish. They may have Irish names, but they don't have the sarcasm or the caustic Irish sense of humor. TV cops believe in good and evil, but Irish people believe in crime and punishment not in rah-rah absolutes. And TV cops don't say the kinds of things I've heard cops say over the years. Here then is how a true Irish cop would confront a suspect. *Law & Order* writers, take note.

> *"Who's this fuckin' cock-knocker? Nimrod over here grabbed his chain, and then this fuckin' winner calls over fuckin' Robert Moses to redesign the building. Then you got Stephen Hawking over here, trying to work out universal theories on his prick. That's who we got here."*

One night in Times Square—back when pimps were lined up on the street like Citi Bikes—when I was twenty-one and drunk by myself in some bar, I found a piece of tinfoil and crafted it into a fake badge to pass for a bloated, middle-aged policeman. So I impersonated a cop. I walked up to a group of young black guys who were out looking for tourists to "vic," as they used to say—"Manhattan make it, Brooklyn take it." I decided, as a new representative of the thin blue line, that I needed to clean up Times Square. "Against the wall!" I demanded, flashing my tinfoil badge. They assumed the position, and then I said, "I'm joking! It's a fake badge!" Most of the guys left, either because they still thought I really was a cop or because they thought I was out of my mind.

But one guy stuck around. "What a good idea!" he said, and then pointed to the corner of the block we were on. "Let's use that trick to go rob those hookers!"

"Ladies!" I said in my best cop voice, holding out my fake badge as we approached them. "Police!"

After that things happened very fast. The women started screaming and smashing me with their bags. This was when I found out that hookers carried weights and rocks in their purses for protection. Within minutes I was lumped up so badly I could barely crawl away. I looked for my partner, but he must have gotten transferred out of the precinct.

Even without the badge, I have policeman-like tendencies. The comic Neal Brennan was telling me the other day about a fight he'd had with his brother. "My brother's not talking to me," Neal said, "because I didn't hire him on *Chappelle's Show*. I mean, he came in and read, but I had to tell him, 'Sorry, Kevin, we're going in a different direction.'"

"Of course he's mad at you!" I said. "You don't use that phrase with your brother! Even with strangers it's pretty shitty, but you definitely don't tell someone you're related to, 'We're going in another direction.' That's horrible. How could you do that to your own brother?"

Neal stared at me, then he said, "You realize, of course, that you just pulled an Irish arrest on me. Instead of just agreeing with me, because I'm your friend and I'm just telling you this story so you will show me some sympathy, you say, 'I call you out on your bad behavior.'"

* * *

When I was new to comedy, there was an Irish Mafia in the Boston comedy world. The first time I met Steve Sweeney, I was presented to him like he was the Godfather. They brought me upstairs to a special table at Nick's, the big Boston comedy club. He was sitting in the back, drinking and doing coke in this dark corner table. I sat at his table and he held court while I tried to keep up.

It dawned on me at some point that he was checking me out to make sure I could work in the city of Boston. It felt like a job interview. Twenty minutes later, I left and wasn't banned from the city, so I guess it went okay. I don't know what would have happened if he hadn't approved my application, but luckily I passed muster.

Lenny Clarke's brother, Mike, was the booker in Boston, so instead of ripping people off like it happened in New York, Boston was a fair city when it came to pay. As a result, the Boston guys made much better money. If I got sixty dollars in New York for a show, I'd get two hundred in Boston—all because Mike Clarke, the original booker, was honest and Irish.

That's another reason I like Irish people: They believe in fair play. Because I've always been paid well there, I tend to feel warm and misty about Boston. But the night after my job interview with Sweeney, things took a turn for the worse. Like a lamb to the slaughter, I was introduced at Nick's Comedy Stop as a guy from New York. I went up there with a good feeling—*These are my people*, I thought. In a matter of minutes, two hundred angry redheaded Southie kids with blond eyebrows were threatening to beat the piss out of me. Everyone there is Irish, so to them I was just a New Yorker. I had to hide in the kitchen while my friend Joe and the bouncers begged those freckle-faced Wahlburgers not to deck-shoe my skull in.

* * *

When I call shotgun, you better let me have shotgun. One night in my twenties, I went out with my friends Chris, Lou, Jay, and Mott. I forget where we went, but it couldn't have been much fun, because before dawn we were all crunched into Jay's little Mustang on our way back to Brooklyn. I was in the back.

To help pass the time, I started to smack Lou, who was in the front seat, with the seat-belt buckle. So somewhere in the East Village he got out of the car and started to walk down the street. Jay starts to follow him in the car, but in his haste to get Lou back in the car he failed to observe that we were going the wrong way on a one-way street...with a police precinct on it.

In a matter of moments, the cops had pulled us over. Jay, normally the most mellow and reasonable fellow even when not intoxicated, rolled down the window and bellowed at the officer in front of it, "*What?!*"

The officer yanked Jay out of the window by his collar and slammed him on the front window of the car. This caused my friend Chris and me to deteriorate into spasms of laughter. We were delusional enough to believe that somehow we were only observers in this situation.

Mott got out of the car, but Chris and I wouldn't budge, even when the cops started trying to pull the front seats up to get us out (it was a two-door). We just held on to those front seats for dear life. Finally the cops managed to drag us out and handcuff us. One of them was smirking, so I started to make sarcastic comments about his appearance. The cop punched me in the stomach. Because I was a kid and had zero body fat and a .35 alcohol level, I just stood there looking at him like I was Harry Houdini. It's still the proudest moment of my life.

The policemen dragged us into the station house and put us into an open cell, from which we could see the detectives' bureau. We spent the whole time fighting with each other and tormenting the 6'6" black dude who was in there with us. I was very brave. It may have had something to do with the fact that he was in six-point restraints and couldn't move a muscle. I kept leaning in his face and saying things like, "You must be a real tough guy. Ha! It's like they put you in a jail cell inside a jail cell!"

He growled unintelligibly, and his eyes said, "I would give all my commissary for the next year for five minutes alone with this scrawny, big-mouthed, brave-when-I'm-in-a-straitjacket white motherfucker." (Black people can always turn absolutely any trait into a compound adjective: "What did this good-mood, new-sneakers, brown-shirt mother-fucker want?")

In that cell that night, I generously shared my powers of observation with the late-shift detective unit. I pointed out that one robust, pink-faced fellow Celt should be an under-cover operative, because from his white socks with black shoes up past his bulging Van Heusen dress shirt, straight through to the broken blood vessels that wound through his nose like a Turkish heroin smugglers' route, he would never be identified as a member of the famously svelte and stylish New York Police Department of the 1980s.

Well, this brought him to the cage. He tried to grab me, but I was protectively plastered against the back wall, because this was not my first time at the rodeo. I knew the arms were going to come through and try to strangle me at some point before I made bail.

Sadly, all good things come to an end. At two in the morn-ing they finally released us—even Jay, who had been driving, blew a miraculously low number on the Breathalyzer. And yet, as we were getting ready to leave the station, we learned that they had impounded Jay's car.

"That's just wrong!" shouted Lou, who had not been locked up but like a good friend had been sitting and drinking coffee for hours at the station house waiting for our release. "You can't do that!"

Suddenly, the desk sergeant reaches behind the desk and whips a roll of toilet paper at Lou, splashing Lou's hot coffee all over his shirt. Lou was temporarily stunned but finally spit out, "What was that for?"

"I thought," the desk sergeant replied, "you might want a roll with your coffee."

This sent the rest of us into gales of laughter at our poor friend's expense. And we kept laughing even as we headed out into the East Village night, into the rain and the dark, for yet another long subway ride home.

* * *

Getting arrested was just part of my life as a self-described Irish intellectual and comic poet. I had read all the works of James Joyce. I read *Ulysses* first and then didn't read the other works but told everybody I did until I felt like I had. I imagined myself as some combination of Joyce, Dylan Thomas, and Yeats, only young and hot.

I obsessively read J. P. Donleavy's books. He was an Irish American novelist and playwright who wrote about angry young men and made drinking heavily seem like an excellent idea. His book *The Ginger Man* is about this guy who's a drunken piece of shit but thinks he's a gentleman. I found it inspiring and reassuring. In my patched jacket, I would go out to the craziest bars in Brooklyn and I thought everyone there saw me and thought, "Oh, he must be a writer."

My father, who also loved these writers, enabled my delusions. His father was from Belfast and died when he was young, and so he had a romantic idea of the literary Irish life. He loved the idea of me being a wild Irish poet-writer. I loved the idea, too. Both of us wanted me to be this guy. My father never said, "Hey, wait a minute, you're just a drunk!"

Another part of my literary persona involved a transient living situation. After my bartending jobs let out I used to crash at a variety of apartments. One was my father's depressing, postage-stamp-size studio apartment, complete with brick-wall view and Ralph Kramden refrigerator. He kept his apartment like a monk's cell as penance for getting divorced. My father taught English at City College. He loved the Brooklyn Dodgers until they abandoned New York, and after that he didn't care about baseball. He was a well-dressed, charming guy, and a bit of a player—which is how he came to be living alone in a penance apartment.

One day on my way to visit my father I had a meeting with my manager, who was going on about this movie called *No Surrender*, about the pointlessness of the fighting between the Irish and the English. "The movie was great," my manager said. "But this old Irish guy in the audience started a fistfight with this young guy behind him."

When I got to my dad's apartment, I saw that his knuckles were bleeding. "What happened?" I asked him.

"These guys were talking behind me at the movies," he said. "And I asked them to stop, and one of them said, 'Shut up, old man.'"

What are the odds? It was a little movie. Probably a thousand people in the whole country saw it, but my father and my manager were at the same showing.

Besides my father's place, I had a few crash pads, including my friend Chris's apartment on 3rd Street in Park Slope. I'd go back to Chris's house all lumped up. He remembers the second half of a lot of stories I have from those days.

I also inhabited a series of temporary apartments on the Lower East Side. Any of the latter would still be mine today if I'd been smarter about real estate. And if I described to you now how casually I relinquished those ridiculously spacious and cheap apartments, five graphic designers who are at this very moment sharing one of my former living rooms on Avenue B would justifiably kill me.

Unfortunately, although I'd made my artistic decision to be an Irish comic poet, my body of work still consisted mainly of walking around in a drunken stupor, dropping cigarettes, and then cursing to myself as I retraced my steps and tried to find them. I was not making much creative progress. I was an actor and writer, but I didn't write or act. I was a bartender, but in my mind I was really the customer. I talked to people, smoked, snuck drinks. I would pontificate while people were waiting for their drinks.

The people I worked for weren't too swift, so they would just say, "I guess he knows what he's talking about," and let me carry on. Those were the days when everyone was hammered. I really loved drinking and smoking. I was also addicted to Regal Crown Sour Cherries, a candy they sadly don't make anymore. I didn't do drugs that often, but I would do coke if people had it. In the early eighties, most conversations were more or less people saying fake things between lines of coke.

One time, I told a girl I was making out with that I had a girlfriend and felt kind of bad about cheating. "I don't care about you and your girlfriend," she said. "I'm not going to pretend that I do." That blew my mind. This was in the eighties, when no one was honest like that. I found it extremely refreshing. And later when I ended things with her she just stood up in the middle of my stupid spiel, gave me a look, and walked away. I never saw her again. Everyone else I encountered back then was pretty coked up all the time. To be fair, it was bad coke, so people didn't get that high. It's hard to get addicted to lint, laxatives, Comet, and baby powder, but not impossible.

Like many gentlemen who spend all their money on alcohol and cigarettes, I had one pair of jeans and one jacket that I thought looked good. I wore them out just as I wore out my welcome. I was in a state of belligerent wretchedness. A member of the landed gentry mistaken for a swollen-faced, pig-eyed menace. I was never helpful and guaranteed to subtract from any situation. I swaggered around like a badass, because I'd taken four judo classes when I was eleven. *Everyone's happy to see me*, I thought when I arrived anywhere.

If you had a kitchen counter, I would sit on it. If you offered me alcohol, I would drink it while sitting on your kitchen counter until I was physically removed. Hints, insults, or threats would only arouse my indignation. I would gladly debate for hours as long as I didn't have to get up and go anywhere else.

I remember one night hanging out at the East Village apartment of a waitress I worked with. I was drunk and stoned and getting ready to make my move on her when who should walk in from his bartending job but her boyfriend—who lived with her. Somehow I had neglected to register that she was not available. Very little useful information penetrated my brain in my drunken state. And yet, one thing was coming through loud and clear: this guy's negative energy.

Why was he displeased? I was baffled. After a hard day of work, what's more reassuring than coming home and finding your girlfriend drinking blackberry brandy and smoking bad pot with a quasi-homeless fill-in bartender?

Well, I decided to disarm him with candor, so I mumbled something along the lines of, "Get the fuck out of here so I can fuck your girlfriend."

Well before you could say "cockblocker," this would-be cuckold cracks me in the side of the head with a very impressive left hook. I scream in justifiable outrage, shock, and pain, and grapple with him to avenge both my honor and that of all misunderstood poet laureates everywhere.

The girl starts screaming. She then surprises me by choosing to help this party crasher out to ruin our fun rather than me, her coworker and potential lover. The night then ended, as so many did in those days, with a sensitive soul bounding down the stairs pursued not just by his own demons but by the pettiness and jealousy of those too small-minded to recognize the great artist in their presence.

* * *

At that time, I was often blindsided by how mad I made women. I've been beaten up by girls more than once in my life. The first time was on North Avenue when I was nineteen and making out with someone at a bar. We went into the back to fool around some more, but then she realized that I'd forgotten her name and called it off. As we were heading back into the bar, another girl starts running at me. She was the sister of the girl, and my friend told her that her sister was in the back "fucking my friend."

"That's my sister!" she yelled at me. "She's only sixteen!" Her friend got behind me and she punched me. I fell over her friend. My friends thought it was *hilarious*.

Another time I was beaten up by girls was when I used to hang out at this bar called One U (for One University Place) in the Village. One night there, two lesbians were competing with me for the same girl. Their weapon of choice was that they were women. My weapon was that I was a mysterious figure from Ireland with a dark past.

In a strong Irish accent, I would make up elaborate tales about "the Troubles" I'd left behind when I came to America, implying that I'd been involved in some high-stakes IRA thing. Or maybe, if I was talking to a guy who seemed to be fascinated by mob stuff (most men are fascinated by mob stuff), I'd make it sound like I had something to do with some dangerous outfit like the Westies, the Irish gang run out of Hell's Kitchen.

"But I'd rather not talk about it," I'd say wearily, staring into the distance and taking another sip of my drink. My alter ego was a heroic, sturdy fellow, just a man trying to mind his business and have a quiet drink (preferably on you).

My grandfather had in fact been in some trouble in Belfast. In my mind, he would have been proud of me for appropriating his life story to hit on girls. *Trinity*, a big book by Leon Uris about Ireland, was very popular in the seventies. I would take parts of the book and parts of what I'd heard about my grandfather's life in Northern Ireland, and some stories from when my father went over in 1982 with the hunger strikers. Many of the quotes I used were actually lyrics from the sixties Irish bands my father liked to listen to, like the Chieftains and the Clancy Brothers.

I combined it all to create this exciting new person named Colum, a two-fisted roustabout. I knew it had to be a name that was close enough to mine so that if I slipped up when

I got blind drunk, which I most certainly would, people wouldn't notice. Colum made a lot of friends arriving in bars and a lot of enemies leaving the bar two hours later.

All night at the bar I would talk about how terrible the English were, and I would refer cryptically to my dangerous life in Ireland with lines like, "It's a terrible situation." (Uris was always talking about "terrible beauty" in *Trinity*.) I would talk about how green it was in Ireland. "It's so beautiful there when it rains," I would say, like the brilliant writer I believed myself to be. I said that in Belfast I'd lived in an apartment in the Divis Flats, which I'd read about somewhere. That was my own research, and I was very proud of that detail. That wasn't my grandfather or my father or *Trinity*. That was all me. I also came up with "Colum," even though it would have been easier to go with *Trinity*'s hero's name, Conor. Not bad, right?

Anyway, I didn't conjure Colum only to pick up girls. I used him *all the time*. Colum was a great, mysterious guy who everyone wanted to have around until he got so drunk he made himself conspicuously unwelcome, even in the diviest of 1980s New York dive bars. Bartenders always knew I was full of shit. They hated me on sight. They never once fell for Colum's stories. They knew the type: Too friendly. Big tip the first round. Just another asshole with a made-up life they'd have to throw out at closing time.

One day, I walked into the Blarney Stone on 42nd Street and Eighth Avenue, one of the run-down, cheap bars that New York was once filled with. They were like neighborhood bars, but for strangers. You would walk in and there was a steam table filled with roast beef and turkey and potatoes. Construction workers and city workers were there from eleven to two. At 4 p.m., the alcoholic business guys about to get fired showed up in their frayed jackets and cheap ties. Then at night, you had pimps and hookers drinking purple and green drinks at the back tables, and assholes like me in the bartender's face. No one went in for just one drink; they went in to wobble out. The death of New York is the death of those bars.

No one is ever turned away. But the bartender who sees me walk in just shouts, "No!"

"What?" I said.

"Out!" he said, exasperated. "No!"

"If you're kicking me out of the *Blarney Stone*," I said, "where am I supposed to go?"

And so our hero Colum went downtown and got beaten up by lesbians, and the girl they were fighting over went home alone.

* * *

My facility for accents wasn't my only means of attracting women. I also had my eyes. A girl once told me I had nice eyes. When I was drunk, I took that to mean I had hypnotic eyes that made Paul Newman's look like a rat's. Some people should not be complimented.

What I would do is I'd start drinking, then I'd walk over to a girl and start working the eyes, hoping that they would

Colin Quinn

put the intended conquest into such a state of arousal that she'd be in the ladies' room bent over a sink before you could say, "Where'd that guy go? He didn't pay for his drinks."

One night my charms worked and I was actually at a girl's apartment, but I felt I was losing her, and so I started working the pupils, the lids, the lashes—the whole thing. Soon, she was guiding me out the door. I whined for an explanation and she said, "Your eyes are a turnoff. They move around too much." To say I was offended would be putting it mildly. This idiot didn't have the aesthetic intelligence to recognize what everybody else knew! I left pitying people who had eyes but couldn't see beauty.

The fact that she got me out of her apartment was a victory in itself. I would fall asleep anywhere, and people would have to throw cold water on me like a cat to wake me up. And that was fine except when I was dressed up. I had three outfits:

1. My friend Mott's Sergeant Pepper jacket with jeans and a form-fitting Löwenbräu T-shirt.
2. Jeans, Timberlands, Members Only jacket.
3. Jeans, Irish sweater, corduroy jacket.

No accessories. Irish don't accessorize. We never have umbrellas, gloves, or sunglasses. Look at a picture of Ireland in the summer. Everyone is walking around squinting. Sunglasses are for people who think they're movie stars. That's why the Irish turned on Bono.

The corduroy jacket was really who I was. That, with my white Irish sweater, let people know that there was a poet in their midst—a man who, though short on cash and drugs, was long on wisdom, advice, and future fortune. This combination played well with the naïve, but any street type would immediately notice the jacket was worn, the sweater was dirty, the bills were all singles, and the cigarettes were all different brands.

No matter. When I walked into a bar you would think that I was walking a runway in Milan in a design that Michael Kors, Armani, Versace, and Gucci had all worked on together. My level of confidence and swagger was somewhere between rapper and bullfighter. I felt that we were all on the same page as a society and that when I came into your place, the party would begin.

When I looked at guys in expensive suits, I would smirk, because I knew they were soulless, spineless drones and I was a true man-about-town. If they had a credit card and I had twenty dollars my mother lent me—well, they needed that credit card to make up for their failings as men. The credit card was a feeble attempt to buy what I had freely given to me: a soaring heart, a keen mind, and the fighting skills of a Green Beret.

I was really proud of these suede boots I had. They were kind of out of style, but my whole identity was wrapped up in those boots—I was an early-eighties, hip, swinging, suede-boots guy, a step ahead of the retro curve. Once I overheard a coworker talking about me, saying, "Him and his fucking stupid suede boots." I yelled at him, "You back-stabbing motherfucker!" They had to hold me back; I was so mad that anyone could not love those boots. It was a real betrayal. I was ready to go to war.

My cap was equally essential to my sense of self. Like Irish guys everywhere, I discovered that I looked very rugged and adventurous when wearing my Irish cap. So wherever I went, I would wear that cap. Considering the amount of blacking out I did, and the places I woke up in (subway cars, jails, highway dividers), it is a minor miracle that I always had my cap when I woke up the next morning.

The one I favored in those years was a corduroy number (paired with my corduroy jacket, it made for a transformative, coordinated look). When I cocked it at an angle most would find over the top and embarrassing, I believed that it set off my blue eyes (which were actually green, but for many years I thought they were blue) in such a way that even the most hard-core lesbian would find me irresistible.

The cap lasted until a black guy up in East Harlem knocked me out. While I was coming to in the Metropolitan Hospital emergency room, two cops asked me who did it.

"A black guy in Harlem," I said. "Does that narrow it down, Baretta?"

They called me a wiseass and left. And when they left, I noticed that my cap was no longer on the chair where I'd seen it minutes before. I wasn't sure if they took my cap to teach me a lesson or as evidence, but as a result I left Metropolitan Hospital not with gratitude for being stitched up (and given a bill that I still haven't paid) but threatening them with a lawsuit if they didn't find my cherished cap.

* * *

One day I put on my famous sweater and decided to go to the landmark old Irish bar McSorley's. It was already something of a tourist trap and I'd already been removed once a year before, but time heals all wounds, and this time I was on a date. I told this girl to meet me there. For some reason they let me in and sat me under a picture of Irish bad-boy writer Brendan Behan, which I thought was a sign that they recognized my talents.

The girl shows up and things start off well, as they always seemed to. As I ramblingly explained to her who Brendan Behan was and how important his writing was and how his tragic drinking ruined his life, she was shaking her head, and I sensed that I was losing her. That's when I realized who was to blame for her lack of interest. Not her, certainly not me. It had to be Brendan Behan.

I start cursing out the bartenders, informing them that Brendan Behan, their idol, was a renowned sodomite, buggerer, and petty criminal, not to mention the worst writer in Ireland. This girl starts crying and shaking her head. I lean over to wipe her tears away, to show my support for whatever is upsetting her. She slaps my hand away and runs out. That really infuriates me.

As I try to follow her, to reassure her that I will protect her from Brendan Behan, the bartenders and their friends intercept me. While they throw me out, I turn around and, in a moment of lucidity, I reach out to shake the hand of an old Irish man. He looks at me without touching my hand and says, "I'd rather be fucked up my arse by Brendan Behan a thousand times than to shake your hand once."

As I was waking up the next morning, the first thing I remembered was that rude man, his terrible comment, and that only Irish drunks will start a fight over a dead writer.

* * *

Colum had many drug-addicted bar acquaintances. One night, Colum was drinking with an escort at Phebe's on the Bowery. She took me with her to meet a drug dealer up on 77th and First Avenue.

While she went into his room and had sex with the dealer, I regaled his two Dominican partners with stories of my life in Belfast. I told them about how I was detained in England and was good friends with the Irish political activist Bernadette Devlin, who they might have heard of? No? Well, we were very close back in the day. She's actually a friend of the family and that's how I got started in the whole terrible mess, I explained. The Brits would set the Protestants loose on us and then arrest us after they burned our houses.

"That's fucked up!" they said.

Dominicans will jump on your side immediately. They lose themselves in the moment. If this girl hadn't come tottering out of the bedroom just then, I could've had these guys beating on the doors of the British embassy with their giant belt buckles.

But the girl and I left and she let me crash at her apartment on the living room couch. She wouldn't fuck me, but that was just as well, because I didn't want to follow the stallion of Santo Domingo, or so I told myself. She said she was going to sleep and went to her room. How she was going to fall asleep after doing that shitload of coke I didn't know, but anyway, as I lay on the couch, in walks the most beautiful blonde girl I've ever seen. She looked like Debbie Harry. On her arm is a loud, annoying suburban business executive right out of central casting.

The girl looks into my beautiful blue eyes and I caught the message: Save me from these horrors. But she still goes into a bedroom. Then another cute girl comes in with another well-heeled gentleman. After a brief how-do-you-do, they go into another bedroom. I realize I'm in the middle of a goddamn brothel, on the couch, pussyless and cokeless in an apartment full of pussy and coke.

I decide that the best way to rescue Blondie is to tell the businessman I'm these young ladies' pimp and he has to pay me a cut. I also decide to tell my Queen of Punk that she should give me some coke and have sex with me. I knock loudly on the door and start describing my demands. The door opens and the girl tells me to get the fuck out or she's going to have me killed. I gave her my best streetwise smirk. (Colum's accent and backstory were long gone by this point; I was all Brooklyn now.) She put her nails on the side of my face and gave me a face rake like I haven't seen since Blackjack Mulligan's claw in the early days of the WWF.

I grabbed my face and ran screaming out into the night. For about a week I had those scratches that appear in every third episode of *Law & Order*, Vincent D'Onofrio saying, "Where'd you get those scratches, Senator?" And the senator says, "Are you accusing me of something, Officer?"

* * *

Often at bars I would focus in on the lonely, fat traveling businessman who wanted a partner while he tried to hook up with chicks in the Big Apple and believed my tales about the girls we would get together.

One night at an after-hours bar, this red-faced ex–football lineman gone to seed from Michigan and I met a beautiful girl who was game for a little action with me. (Who wouldn't be? Go check my Twitter pic @iamcolinquinn. I looked like what McConaughey thinks he looks like.)

Michigan tries to horn in on the action. He thinks that because he has an apartment nearby, he has right of first refusal. After finally giving up, he gives me the keys to his corporate apartment. He tells me when we're done to come back to the bar and get him. The girl and I go back to his place and later I end the night walking her home through a romantic New York dawn. I woke up back at my place alone…with Michigan's keys.

The worst thing about being a drunk is that every day, the number of places you can never return to rises. And yet at the same time, you forget which places you can never go back to without getting an ass-kicking, so you end up back at them without even realizing how much danger you're in. If I had a nickel for every time I said "Oh fuck" during those days, I'd be a rich man.

Two nights later I'm back at the after-hours club and I see this furious face looking at me. I only vaguely remembered him and the whole incident, so I blew it off. I go in the bathroom to take a piss, and the next thing I know I'm being choked to death at a urinal by someone so dumb he doesn't carry spare keys. The only thing that saved my life that time was that the people who were doing coke in one of the stalls came out and dragged those Great Lakes paddles off my throat.

* * *

Around this time, I began to give every woman I was interested in the same book: John Kennedy Toole's *A Confederacy of Dunces*. The Pulitzer Prize–winning novel about a messed-up, hunter's-cap-wearing New Orleans man named Ignatius J. Reilly is my favorite book. It has saved me from killing myself on several occasions. If the woman I wanted to date didn't read it, or didn't like it, I knew the relationship was going nowhere.

Now, of course, if someone did that to me, gave me a *book* as a *test*, I'd be like, "Test me? Fuck you. I'm going to hate this on principle." But at the time I found it very romantic. It went hand in hand with what I considered my

Colin Quinn

very sophisticated lifestyle: working in restaurants with Mexicans, fighting with Arab cabdrivers, and imagining myself as living a true Irish poet's life. I had always been a method customer at bars. In Alphabet City, I would get drunk in old-man Spanish bars and speak Spanish-sounding gibberish. "Corendo, amigo!" I would say in a friendly voice. "Vachaca!" And in the Ukrainian bars, I thought I was speaking Ukrainian. "Prechta!" I would call out in a vaguely Slavic tone. "Sprchetchana!" Everywhere I went, the regulars would just glower at me, this dope sitting in the corner, making up words, but I felt very cosmopolitan.

I drank at the Holiday Lounge on St. Marks Place for a couple of weeks straight, until a biker guy kissed me full on the lips out of nowhere and then, after I said I wasn't into it, threatened to kill me. I just shrugged and found another bar. At some point during this time I woke up on a flea-ridden bed at the notorious St. Marks Hotel and raced out of there rather than risk the creepy shower.

I woke up on the famously drunken Bowery three times— a couple of those in flophouses and once in the actual gutter. At the flophouses, I told my bunkmates that I was from Missouri and had been riding the rails. The cops had beaten me up, and that's how I'd wound up there, down on my luck. Now that I recall these escapades, I realize that most of the lies I told were ripped straight out of 1920s literature. I wonder how many bums came across *The Grapes of Wrath* later and were like, "Wait a minute..." Or, who knows, maybe they thought, "Huh, this must be based on that guy I met!"

* * *

While I'm confessing my sins—another hard-to-break Irish habit—I never went out of my way to steal anything, but I was amoral, and I would take an opportunity if one presented itself. This being the seventies and early-eighties bar scene, the level of security wasn't what it would be later, and so I was presented with a lot of opportunities, and as a result I robbed a lot of shit.

One night, drinking at a Spanish bar after a waiter shift nearby, I came up with a great plan. I'd been drinking there for hours and I was out of money. Sitting next to me was a drunk Puerto Rican guy, my new best friend, and he was also out of money.

"What are we going to do?" he asked, because clearly calling it a night wasn't an option.

It hit me like a light, the greatest idea ever: I stood up and pointed to a guy with forty dollars sitting there in front of him and said, with a swell of indignation, "That was my twenty dollars! I was going to leave that as a tip!"

This was a bold move in a bar that rough. The bar didn't need bouncers, because everyone drinking there looked like a bouncer.

The bartender looked at me, and then said the worst thing he could have said: "How dare you? That guy is my best friend."

At this point, my Puerto Rican friend jumps off the barstool, turns his back, and starts shadow boxing, as if preparing for the fight of his life. "This guy's a boxer!" I said, going with the improv routine, and thinking maybe he even was a boxer and we'd be okay. "He'll fuck you up!" I added, optimistically.

The bartender, the guy I'd accused of stealing, and all their bounceresque friends came rushing us, and my friend—who, as it turned out, was no boxer—and I ran for our lives.

Whenever I heard about there being no exit strategy in the Iraq War, I thought of that night. We got a head start and made it to the exit fast. I was pretty sure we were going to make it. We burst through the first set of double doors, no problem. Then we hit the second one, hard. The second set was locked. Chained up. We turned around and were met with a flurry of fists.

My night ended as they so often did in those days, at 7:30 in the morning, walking down the street boiling hot in my ripped waiter uniform—black pants and white shirt—all bloody and beaten up, passing everyone else on their way to work.

Hypocritically, I had no patience for other people stealing.

I worked at one bar on the Upper East Side that was owned by a famous Irish badass thug everyone was scared of. One of the bartenders was stealing. One day, the owner says to the thief, "C'mere for a second." Then, without warning or explanation, he punched him in the face. The guy fell down, out cold, behind the bar. He did this in front of the customers. I thought that was brilliant.

One time, I was bartending and this waiter kept chiseling me on tips. And so I did what any reasonable person would do in that situation: I went to the bank and took out twenty dollars in pennies. At the start of that day's lunch shift, I went up to the crook and said, "Hey! I forgot to give you your change from last week." And then I poured the pennies on his head and started punching him.

We had to go before some kind of restaurant board. I was genuinely shocked when they fired me and kept him.

* * *

Another thing, Father. Cabdriver fights: I had four that I remember. I can't blame the drivers; I was drunk all the time. Once on 20th Street and First Avenue, I got mad because the guy wouldn't take me to Brooklyn. This was the early eighties, when that happened even more than it does now. So I start yelling. Well, all the other cabbies on First Avenue pulled over and started beating me over the head with the extensive arsenal of rubber-covered tire irons they carried on their front seats. I was screaming, but I could appreciate the unity of it, if it wasn't me being pummeled. The cops showed up and arrested *me*, the injured party!

I have been arrested five or six times. Once while I was in college at Stony Brook, and the other times in Manhattan. And it was during this auspicious, jail-rich period that I started my career in comedy.

One Sunday morning, around noon, I woke up in the gutter in Times Square. I decided then and there that it was time to get serious about stand-up. "I'm going to the Improv," I vowed, "and I'm signing up." I was still drunk from the night before. The guy at the Improv said, "Come back in four hours."

What could I do with four hours? I went to the bar and started drinking again. Then I was tired. What was I going to do to wake up? I decided to buy some coke. I found a guy to sell me some and followed him into a building. All of a sudden, there are four cops rushing in doing "the matinee sweep."

They took me to the Times Square police substation.

"Let me go!" I pleaded. "This is bullshit! I'm a comedian. I have a set to do!"

"You're a comedian?" a cop said. "Okay. Entertain us. Do your set."

They set me up on a riser and told me to perform. I did five minutes for the cops and about twenty kids who'd just been arrested. It was my first comedy show ever. I didn't get one single laugh. It was the worst anyone has ever bombed, anywhere.

"We were going to let you go because you said you were a comedian," one of the cops said, "but now we know you were lying."

* * *

My first performance at a comedy club didn't actually go all that much better. Pips Comedy Club was in Sheeps-head Bay, which at the time was all blue-collar Italians and

Jews. There were two bars out there: Captain Walters and Wheeler's. Going there was like making the hippest scene. If someone asked, "Have you been to Captain Walters?" and you said, "Sure, I was there last week!" everyone would say, "Ooh!" It was like Studio 54 for that part of Brooklyn. It was nerve-racking going there, because there was an actual bouncer and a rope. Even though you were seventeen with a fake ID that made you eighteen and which they never looked at too closely anyway, when you got in you really felt like an adult. It was a prestigious thing to get in, although, now that I think about it, they never really turned anyone away.

And the other place we wanted to get into was Pips Comedy Club. Wednesday night was audition night. The first time I showed up, I saw a sign out front: "Nick Tantino will not be performing tonight."

"Shit, they need me!" I thought joyfully, even though I'd never heard of Nick Tantino.

I walked in and went onstage to do my set in front of a crowd of ten people. Right after I start, twenty Italian skinhead guys from Avenue X run in with their cut-off T-shirts and start throwing chairs and chasing everyone out of the club. "The real show is outside!" they kept yelling.

I immediately ran to the side of the owners, Seth and George Schultz, and stood with them, because I wanted a gig and figured if I backed them up, kissed their ass by taking a beating, maybe they'd have me back. I followed them outside to see what was going on. When we got there, we saw Nick Tantino standing on the back of a flatbed truck with a microphone, doing his routine. The owners had rejected Tantino, and he and his friends had set up the sign and the flatbed club as payback.

Half of the people who'd been in the club went home, and the other half stood around the truck laughing at his jokes. They seemed totally unfazed, like, "Okay, I guess the show's out here now," as if it was totally normal for a gang to throw them out of one club and present an alternative that required them to stand on the sidewalk. That's when I should have left the business—seeing that half a crowd would think a flatbed truck comedy club made total sense.

But my loyalty to the Schultzes paid off. I went back Friday night to perform, a real spot. Unfortunately, I bombed. I was too green. When you start out, you have your whole act memorized, every second of it. And as you say it all out loud there's something uncomfortable in the air. Your body, your voice, are just awkward. And you have this sense like something's missing. That's because doing the show over and over in your head you've left space for laughs. When you're performing, you see with crystal clarity all the places where you're waiting for the laugh and it doesn't come. If—when—they don't laugh, it throws you off. "Wait," you want to say to them, "you sitting here quietly isn't part of the plan."

* * *

One of my bartending jobs during this period of time was at a place called the Cookery on University and Eighth Street. This old guy Bob was the cook. I would slip him vodka all night. One night, after about seven greyhounds, he said, "We should go to Brownsville." And so I went along with him to an after-hours club he knew.

This was 1981. Brownsville, Brooklyn, was one of the more dangerous neighborhoods in America back then. They wouldn't let us in the club, because I was white. They thought I was a cop. Bob was outraged. As a white person in a black neighborhood, you're under your black friends' protection. If you die, they have to die with you.

Even as drunk as I was, I was thinking, "This is the worst idea, yelling at an after-hours bouncer on the street where they used to bully Mike Tyson."

I'm not sure what happened next, but I ended up walking around Brownsville by myself. Kids were yelling at me. I was yelling back. But back then I had no fear. I carried myself a certain way. Talk about beer muscles. When I drank, I was convinced I was an intellectual martial arts champion. I swaggered around the streets of New York City like I owned them. I'd just walk into bars and start barking orders. Running through my mind a lot back then were mantras like, *I hope that guy tries something. I really hope he tries something.*

It was a good thing I had a mustache back then. That mustache probably saved my life twenty times just that night in Brownsville alone. Even though I was only twenty-two, everyone thought I was a cop. It was a Tom Selleck mustache and, especially combined with my short haircut, it made me look like Nick Nolte in that 1990 movie *Q & A*.

Sometimes I'd get tested and someone would knock me out. Every time I got beat up, I'd say, "Of course! I was so drunk." But most of the time tough guys would say, "Wow, I don't want to mess with that guy. Look at that mustache!" That night in Brownsville, I woke up lying in this grassy patch of an outdoor train station next to three homeless people. I had to beg money to get on the train. That was all part of my romantic rejection of society's values.

One time, I ended up with this chick in the projects of East Orange, New Jersey. I swaggered through them like the white Treach. That girls had balls, too. What's she doing bringing a white guy to the projects? When I woke up the next morning in her bed, it was raining. On the radio was the violinist Jean-Luc Ponty, who was big in the seventies. I remember thinking, *What a sophisticate I am!* We were in bed in New Jersey and I was smoking a cigarette listening to Jean-Luc Ponty. I thought I was living in a movie. Sure, I was going to have to beg change to get train fare back home, but in my mind we were on the Left Bank of Paris in 1958.

Another time I went drinking in the now-hip, then-empty Brooklyn neighborhood of Williamsburg. The next morning I woke up and there was noise. I had a hangover. I thought, *I have to shut the window.* I stood up and it turned out I had fallen asleep on the median of the Brooklyn-Queens Expressway.

To make matters worse, my family was driving out to Long Island for a visit that morning and my mother saw me walking along the road, clearly still drunk from the night before.

"That was Colin," she said, and made them turn around to go find me. But by the time they turned the car around I was gone. She saw me a few days later and said, "The other morning, were you walking along the highway in Brooklyn?"

"No," I said.

But she knew. My grandmother knew it, too.

* * *

They say prisoners of war have to make up things to get by. I have no excuse for being such a delusional person. I've developed a theory: Delusion is something you need to be in show business. You definitely need it in comedy. It takes a certain amount of delusional thinking to go to places in Ohio or Colorado and walk onstage with nothing—no instrument, no props—and say, "I deserve to get paid for this, just standing here talking about whatever comes into my head."

This is a constant for my whole life. In 1991, I would be fired from a TV show built around me and my life. Maybe my firing had something to do with the fact that I had recently given notes to the director, who had flowing blond Viking hair and was the hottest director in Hollywood. "This script isn't funny and doesn't make any sense," I'd said while surrounded by Gothic furniture in some huge tower building. "Those are very serious charges," he'd said, tossing his Scandinavian locks.

Peter Chernin, the head guy and a big deal even then, said while he was firing me, "I never say this"—in my mind I thought, *He always says this*—"but I feel like I'm going to regret letting you go." My only thought was, "That's a given." My delusions of grandeur made me fully impervious to the sting of rejection.

An inflated sense of my own importance killed me in some ways and saved me in others. The first time I went to the comedy club Catch a Rising Star, I was kicked out of the line for being drunk. "You're gonna pay for this," I said, as I was being dragged away from the door. "I'm funnier than everyone else here!"

When I returned to Catch to perform, I was never intimidated, although back then you had these huge names performing on the same bill as you, even when you were really green. Someone like Rodney Dangerfield would go on and kill, changing the whole energy of the room, and afterward the host would say, "Who wants to go next?" and every single comic, even the newest one, would say, "I'll go on!"

One time, I was in Pittsburgh at a hotel and the concierge told me he was starting a career in stand-up. As I'd been in the business quite a while by then, I started giving him advice. He cut me off and said, "Yeah, yeah, yeah; I got it." He thought of us as equals. He didn't want advice. Even though he'd probably only done a handful of shows, he must have been a comic because he had it all figured out.

That's how we are. When I was young and saw the

Boston comic Lenny Clarke perform, I went up to him afterward and said, "I'm gonna be a comedian, too." We talked for a bit. I said, "You were funny, but everyone else was terrible." And then I went on to give my unvarnished opinion about what everyone else—some of them comics who had been performing longer than I had been alive—was doing wrong.

"You're right," he said, hearing the obnoxious overconfidence in my voice. "You are going to be a comedian."

* * *

When I quit drinking, it was like losing my best friend in the world. I spent that first sober St. Patrick's Day in my apartment, watching the parade on TV, crying my eyes out. I loved bars so much. All week I would be in a great mood, looking forward to going out—by Friday I'd be soaring—even though it never ended well.

Eventually, twenty-two years ago, I quit smoking, too. I decided I would embrace the misery: Get fat and go crazy. I'm not jealous of very many people, but I wished I could trade places with those old Irish guys who had apparently gotten away with smoking and drinking as much as they wanted for fifty-plus years.

I wasn't one of those guys where his friends are like, "Oh, did you really need to quit? Maybe you could still drink socially." Not one person said anything like that to me when they heard I quit drinking. What they said was, "About time."

I wondered what I would do for excitement now that I wasn't waking up in weird parts of the city covered in bruises anymore. The comedian Doug Stanhope, a famous drinker, once said to me of getting sober, "That's the problem: You quit drinking and then no more good stories, right?"

* * *

We Irish are no longer really a group. We had a wave of popularity from 1920 to 1960. That's over, except in Boston and maybe two neighborhoods in the Bronx. But that's okay, because we know that no matter how much we hate the Catholic Church, they're right about the afterlife and the pain and torment of hell. That's the only logical reason that assholes could do so well in this life. So take comfort and solace in the fact that everybody else is going to be caught looking when they die.

As Colum would say, "The worst were filled with passionate intensity, the best lacked all conviction." Did he steal it from W. B. Yeats? That's your opinion. Now are you going to buy a round or not?

VI

Quiet Ochre

IMMIGRANT ASIANS PUT IN THE HOURS. INDIANS, ASIANS, AND Mexicans are competing for who can sleep the least. If you say one of them looks well rested, they'll take it as an insult. Indians sleep five hours a night and Mexicans sleep four, but Asians sleep three. Asians sleep at work standing up. They can work in their sleep, standing at the cash register.

Koreans are organized. Decades ago, twenty Koreans formed the Korean-American Grocers Association of New York and now there are four thousand members. One woman, Youngja Kim Lee, was apparently the driving force behind nail salons being a Korean business. It's part of their culture to massage elderly relatives' hands, and then it just became their thing.

They're efficient. When you start to ramble, Asians will

149

look at you like, "Do bees stop to bullshit when they're building a hive? Get on with it already."

Chinese people don't like to turn on the charm. They'll never give you the time of day. They don't like to waste smiles, and they're not big on small talk. Ask an Asian, "How're you doing?" They look straight ahead and say, "Fine." There's no Mandarin word for "oversharing." I don't think there's a Cantonese expression for "too much information."

You don't go to China and see a lot of bro-hugging and backslapping. They wear masks and hold their phones in front of them to ward off unwanted contact. They don't trust humans as much as they do technology. The way Italians feel about cars, this is how Asians feel about technology.

People in Asia live in close quarters. Even the rich people live in tenements with their laundry on the line. Laundry hangs on lines along the highways, like electric wires. It's an alternate version of GPS: Make a right at the green shirt and a left at the blue pants.

Asians live in a very closed society and nobody is allowed to complain or be alone for more than ten minutes. Everybody is packed in, and if you want some alone time that's what death is for. They're very nontouchy. I think it's because over there you are constantly rubbing up against each other on the subway, on the street, and in the house.

In America they tell you you're special. That's basically what the Declaration of Independence and the Constitution say. In China they tell you you're a cog. You're special? There's no one like you? Sure. There's no other number 1531 on the conveyor belt at the factory. Only you.

There's no therapist, only the supervisor. Chinese men don't cry, they grunt. If they have an emotional problem, they grit their teeth and smoke eleven cigarettes while making a guttural sound that expresses the depth of their indignation and misery in less than a syllable. That's why smoking is still allowed in China—because it helps you stuff your feelings. Even the sports they indulge in are intense and quiet: Ping-Pong™, billiards, video games.

If an Asian starts to gossip, everyone looks at him like, "Don't you have homework?" They're not allowed to joke around. I've read a lot of Chinese joke books—well, two and a half Chinese joke books—and all the jokes have a philosophical point. Not even their jokes can be mind-less fun.

There are funny Asian comics, and I always imagine it must have taken superhuman strength for them to get past that shame of having to face your relatives at every impor-tant extended-family get-together (these are held every two weeks) and watch your embarrassed parents explain that their child is not a doctor but rather a laugh elicitor in an alcohol hut.

Asians don't ever ask for favors. There's no, "Excuse me, can you change seats with me so I can sit next to my friend?" It's a Spartan life. I often wonder how the hell they tolerate life in this country of complaint, what they think when they hear us bellyaching. Chinese people must be looking at America like it's an interminable kids' play they wish they could walk out on.

* * *

I tip heavily, far more than 20 percent always, and usually more like 50–100 percent. I tip a lot because of my many years in the service industry, as a bartender, and even before that as a Chinese-food delivery boy for the Gongs. In my neighborhood, the legendary Gong family was as badass as anyone got: killer athletes and tough street fighters. Everybody respected them. To other Chinese kids, they were gods.

It was a time when a lot of people tried to make jokes about Chinese people—imitate the way they talked, the way they looked. Nobody did that with the Gongs. They just looked at them and started to say something like, "Hey, Ching Chong. Hey, Kung Fu," but something would stop them. It was the hands that were bigger than they should've been. They were from generations of laborers, born with farmer muscles and calloused feet. The Gongs would go in a minute.

Working at their restaurant, Chim's, was the first time I saw the Chinese work ethic in practice. From open till close, they'd be cleaning, cooking, and smoking. No breaks. In those days you could light up indoors so nobody needed a smoke break. People wonder why production is down in this country and why China is beating us. Because they allow their employees to smoke while they work.

Delivering Chinese food, I went to the poorest and the richest houses in Park Slope. Everyone back then loved Chinese food and found it exotic. And everyone found the efficiency of the customer service incredibly impressive. To this day, New York's Chinese restaurants always have the fastest, most efficient waiters. They're not moonlighting in Off-Off-Broadway theaters or auditioning for commercials. They take out all their anger yelling in the kitchen and then they get you your food without emotion. Have you ever walked out of a Chinese restaurant saying, "Well, I just loved our server!" But you got your food fast, didn't you?

After my time with the Gongs, I worked more delivery jobs, including as a helper for a pet-store driver, shuttling cases of dog and cat food for every hoarder and cat lady in Manhattan (and a couple of cat guys and, yes, they were as creepy as that sounds), and transporting liquor to the alcoholics of Brooklyn for Shawn's Wine & Spirits.

Delivering booze exposed me to another vanished New York archetype: the chronic old-lady alcoholic in the model of Norma Desmond or Miss Havisham. I would knock on the door of some dissipated old floozy who once ran around with Al Capone's cousin or something. They were always happy to see me. It was the same thing when I later bartended. When I was a waiter, people treated me like a class-A nitwit, but when you have control of the alcohol, people are very reverent until they get a few drinks, and then they turn on you. They go from polite banterers to snarling hounds in a matter of three or four kamikazes.

One of the many benefits I had as a delivery boy was that I enjoyed being in people's homes, and they enjoyed hosting a young, friendly fellow (carrying a case of plastic Popov vodka bottles). I was usually in a good mood in those days, which was possibly because I was working my way through a "lid," as we called it, of pretty good pot. In fact, I was rarely without a joint or a cigarette in my mouth.

Delivering cat food and booze to strange homes was both formative and distorting—although to blame my twisted psyche on those soul-destroyed cat ladies and aging former Rockettes of Brooklyn would be blaming the victim, as we say in sociological circles.

One customer was a merry widow who had once perhaps been a blushing flower but was now in the twilight of her years, and her apartment had the gentility of an antebellum-South sitting room combined with the studio apartment of a recently paroled serial rapist. When you walked in, your feet felt like the carpet was moving because of the flotsam and bacilli that had been living there since before the invention of the vacuum cleaner.

But I braved it. She was good for about a gallon of Four Roses bourbon twice a week. People who have liquor delivered don't play games with pints or bottles of the new cabernet or any of that. To them, a liter is an airplane bottle. They need industrial sizes, because they are battling decades of regret and pain and only hope to pass out before the night terrors get them.

But this old bird still had a little spunk left in her. One

day she greeted me in her finest lingerie—which in her case was a sherry-stained robe from a long-closed hotel and a pair of heels that she'd likely bought when she was Miss Subway for the Union Pacific. But she was leaning over, writing me a bad check for a gallon of Gordon's gin, and as men throughout time have done, I was looking down her half-opened robe.

If you've ever read *The Catcher in the Rye*, you might remember Holden catching a glimpse of his favorite teacher's wife's withered breast. Only in my case the hero was far from depressed but in fact becoming quite aroused by the pendulous swaying and rhyme of the ancient *mammariners* that were undulating before his THC-enlarged pupils. I have to give myself credit. I was a lot of things as a youth, but never an ageist.

I took her lack of modesty to be an invitation, so I reached over and put my hand down her blouse. Let me repeat: I reached over and put my hand down her blouse. There was a beat and then she sucked in her breath, which I took as a green light.

Well, apparently there's a reason I failed my first written driver's test, because it was closer to a flashing red. This doddering cocktease, the onetime handjob queen of Ebbets Field, released her breath in the form of a Chesterfield-clotted screech. She started muttering a flashback of the last erotic moment she'd enjoyed (possibly Glenn Miller banging her on a mountain of war bonds while she was wearing a jaunty sailor's cap).

But the ship had sailed long ago. The gangplank pulled up on this wharf rat, and while I was feeling her tits she started wheezing and coughing. Being the gentleman I was, I stopped. She pointed to the bottle, so I poured her a drink and held it up to her lipstick-smeared mouth. (If you want a visual, see Cheri Oteri as Collette Reardon, *Saturday Night Live*, 1997–99.)

As this emphysema-riddled crone sucked on the drink, I continued to gaze at these melons, which—though no longer ripe—had once bounced through the kitchen entrance of the Copacabana with Henry Hill. Let's end this sad story on this image, what they call in fine literature a "tableau": a teenage bum admiring two deflated speed bags from a long-abandoned boxing gym, and a soused floozy whose luck ran out during the Kennedy administration. It brings to mind the Franz Kafka quote, "Youth is happy because it has the capacity to see beauty. Anyone who keeps the ability to see beauty never grows old." The same may be said of anyone who keeps the ability to be turned on by breasts under even the most depressing circumstances.

Anyway, I realized that the stoic Asian temperament was better suited to this kind of emotionally fraught work, and so I quit and found employment elsewhere.

* * *

As a young man, I studied martial arts. And by "studied" I mean I went to judo four times. Karate didn't arrive in America till the movie *The Chinese Connection* (*Fist of Fury*) in

1972. After that movie, street fights changed. Every fight, one kid would throw a karate kick and that would be a crowd-pleaser. It would send everybody laughing and applauding and running around the street like, "Ohhhhhhhhh shiiiiit." Suddenly, people were carrying nunchucks and everybody started asking what belt you were. Being Chinese became cool. You'd see black, white, and Puerto Rican kids wearing those pajamas and slippers, and you knew they were serious martial arts students. They started to talk spiritually: *Water flows, I am the wind, I love my enemy so he defeats himself.* You know the deal: Anybody that has to keep reminding you how peaceful they are is usually a psycho looking to put their fingers through your windpipe.

The TV show *Kung Fu* became popular, even though David Carradine had no Asian blood whatsoever. But because his eyes had an almost Asian caste to them, Hollywood was like, "He looks Asian. We're not going to hire a real Asian to play the part, are we?" Bruce Lee was the only Asian allowed to be famous. We all had the Bruce Lee poster on our walls. We all looked in the mirror and tried to push our lats out. Everybody wanted to learn how to pull someone's still-beating heart out or administer a pressure-point deathblow. And that's what happened to Bruce Lee, as we all knew. He died because he revealed the kung fu secrets to Westerners. At a sparring session, a Shaolin monk delivered a delay blow that killed him a few days later, but it looked like natural causes. Or maybe it was a cerebral edema.

The way martial arts classes worked was this:

The first thing that happens is they charge you forty bucks for your uniform.

Then they teach you how to count to ten in Chinese.

Then they pair you off with somebody to spar with. I always got the short muscular guy with a Napoleon complex who was terrible at life but great at athletics. He'd been studying for about two years and he wanted to prove something to the teacher and the world. He wanted to show all the tall people that he is worthwhile and he wanted to make an example of me. I'd be trying to learn a new wrist hold and he was going after my eye sockets with his fingers.

Then you become an expert on martial arts after two lessons and one karate magazine. And so you get to say things to your friends like, "Yeah, you know, Eagle Claw is bullshit. Sensei says so."

The guys all talked about it like they were experts: "Nah, you have to kick with the *side* of the foot. Then you lock up his wrist like this. See that guy's arms? I would just take him under, take out his knees. I would just grab him like *this*. Then he grabs your wrist, then I would twist it like this…"

And someone asked, "How long did you study?"

And then you'd have to say, "Two weeks. But my brother is a third-degree black belt, and he showed me."

Now they teach karate at all the health clubs. It's harder to be tough when you study at the gym. Because you used to be able to say, "I studied at Master Woo's Praying Tiger School in a rickety tenement in Chinatown." The names were always the best: Long Fist Kung Fu, Five Animals, Iron Palm Shootfighting, North Filipino Grappling, Mongolian Shin Stomping, Whooping Crane Dirty Fighting.

Now it's, "I take aerobic kickboxing at Bodies in Motion with Sensei Steve." Sensei Steve says, "In this class we will go to the heart of power and fear. Listen, people, somebody is talking shit about you right now. What's your name, buddy?...Bob? Bob, right now there is somebody from the job...Where do you work, Bob?...Right. Bob, right now there is somebody in your engineering firm saying to his friend, 'Bob's drafting is not very precise.' Are you going to take that lying down? That's right, you're not! By the way, if you like this class, you may also enjoy my other courses: Ninjitsu Talking Your Way Out of It and Balinese Blaming the Guy Who's Not There to Defend Himself."

I belong to this gym now where they have all these registered instructors with these complicated workouts they insist are the best. The trainers have so much hype around them: "He was a sparring partner with Oscar De La Hoya." To me that means he probably bumped into De La Hoya at a bar in East L.A. and De La Hoya kicked his ass. "He is an award-winning kickboxer!" That, to me, means he got his green belt from a mini-mall karate school that is now a nail salon.

* * *

The Chinese in New York in the seventies spoke Cantonese and they were from Hong Kong. In the late eighties, all these other Chinese came in that spoke Mandarin and Fukienese, and I always wondered how the interactions went. I'm sure it makes you feel good to see more people who look like you and are from the old country. But at the same time, these new people speak a different language, and now you're responsible for them in some way. They're looking to you for guidance, because it's scary to be in a new place. What was that like? But we'll never know because the Chinese are not very forthcoming.

By 1990, instead of Chinatown there was Chinatown and Brooklyn Chinatown and three Queens Chinatowns. The Koreans who'd come in the seventies started to move out to get away from all the Chinese, because Koreans are actually a whole different culture. They like nice cars and nice clothes, whereas a true Chinese person thinks that if you buy a ten-dollar bag to lug things around instead of using a plastic bag, you're a diva. If you need more than one coat and one pair of shoes, you're high maintenance. There are no designer labels allowed. They won't even wear fake designer clothes that they themselves sell on Canal Street.

* * *

The Indians and Pakistanis got here from South Asia around '83, I want to say. That's a guess; I'm not even going to Google it. The Indians moved to Jackson Heights. From there they spread out to Long Island and Edison, New Jersey. And the Pakistanis all moved to Kensington, Brooklyn.

There weren't many Indian kids when I was young, but

when we visited my cousins in Kew Gardens they had a friend called Bimla Dindial. I just told that pointless story because I love to say her name. Everyone in my family loves to say it to this day. Bimla, if you had any idea how much pleasure you've given us over the years, you'd be thoroughly creeped out.

The Indians and Pakistanis took over the newsstands and candy stores from the Jews. Outside the city they ran 7-Elevens, and now New York City has 7-Elevens, which is the final deathblow. I knew NY was finished when I came back from a two-year stint in L.A. in '93 and there was a Domino's Pizza on Coney Island Avenue. I swear to God, I almost started crying.

There was an Indian newsstand guy near my house. I thought we were friends and got each other. Then one day he said, "I save one magazine for you!" It was the gay magazine *Blueboy*. He thought he was being nice and acknowledging what he thought of as my obvious gayness. In fairness, I had a pretty serious mustache, but until that moment I thought it made me look, like, incredibly straight and macho.

I would love to be a fly on the wall at the training session for a recently immigrated news merchant. He just arrived, and his uncle is explaining all the characteristics and peculiarities that each American group exhibits when they come in the store—how they interact, what they purchase. "When you ID drunk for cigarettes, they will call you dothead, and when you ID them for beer they will call you bin Laden. Don't respond."

The tech boom was the best thing to happen to Indians. Why are they so good at this tech support stuff? Not just because they're computer savvy. They're also polite. That was what collapsed the British empire. They were too polite. Every other colony used violence to attain freedom. The Indians' form of revolution was awkward silence until the British showed themselves out.

And they're formal. Talk to any Indian in America or India and they have a beautiful British accent and they still use honorifics like "Sir" or "Miss." Their speech is impeccable, their manners from the Victorian era, and they still wear dress pants. They have a vocabulary that makes our constant "whatevers," "you knows," "likes," and profanity seem juvenile. Indians don't curse and they don't wear jeans. Why wouldn't you want to hire them for every job?

Indians are New Yorkers now, too. They used to be the friendliest people of us all, but now they're just as bitter and sarcastic as the rest of us. Because everybody picked on the Indians when they first came over. Assholes would come in and make fun of the Indian accent.

DRUNK WHITE KID [*wasted, starts harassing the Indian clerk*]: "Hey, Ali Baba."

INDIAN CLERK: "Sir, I must ask you to leave. You are a hindrance to commerce."

DRUNK KID: "Who you calling a hindrance? You're the damn Hindu-rance, not me."

INDIAN CLERK: "Sir, there are other patrons in this queue. You must discontinue this coarse vulgarity."

[*The police arrive. Cop asks what's going on.*]

INDIAN CLERK: "I will tell you precisely what happened, sir. I asked this gentleman to lower his voice of boisterous turbulence. I will add that this man was discourteous and transgressed the queue."

COP: "The what?"

INDIAN CLERK: "The queue of patrons."

COP: "What, like the line?"

INDIAN CLERK: "Yes, sir. The line. The gentleman then picked up an object and used discourteous language that I may not repeat, but I will tell you it began with a most troublesome verb. Subject, object, verb. Adjective. Preposition. Please remove him forthwith."

[*Then the cops write it up and their sergeant yells at them because he needed a thesaurus to read it.*]

Pakistanis are often mistaken for Indians due to the fact that they were technically Indians until around 1947. Because most of them are Muslims, they're a little more "temperamental" than Indian Indians, and they have thicker mustaches. They are not big, but they can be eager to fight.

If you ever get into an altercation with a peaceful Indian and he suddenly punches you in the face, he was probably a Pakistani.

In New York, they always had the friendly guy up front working the candy counter and the hatchet man working the lotto machine. "Sir, you say Cash for Life, not Powerball. I don't make mistake."

They do a lot of brickwork in the Tri-State area, especially on brick row houses in bourgeois Brooklyn, which strikes me as a step up from Islamabad. Then again, the only images I usually see of Islamabad are of ruined houses, before which are standing a thousand disgruntled former allies holding a Zippo to a U.S. flag. Do you think the guy who runs the flammable-American-flag-making company in Pakistan sits around all day hoping for a drone attack so he can move some product?

When Indians die they make funeral pyres. That's what we should be doing, too. Not cremating, which is depressing. A bonfire. That's the way to make an exit. A little glamour, please! You just died! It's a big event.

A muttering priest and three guys with shovels is not the way I'd like to go out, thank you. And let's face it: Putting all these dead bodies in the earth that we have to live on is kind of unsanitary. It's crowding up the earth, and we need that space. Unless we leave the bodies there on the long shot that someday science will invent a way to bring us back, and we'll go to the graveyard to reclaim our people. All these zombies walking out of their graves and their families are sitting in Chevy Suburbans waiting for them like parents picking kids up from camp.

Meanwhile, the Indians are all cows and butterflies, not stacked on top like rotting Hollywood squares.

* * *

Asians, liven up a little. Smile once in a while. Yes, you've got the work ethic that we need to get back to. Yes, you never complain and you are underappreciated. Would it kill you to backslap every once in a while? That's how it works here. Squeaky wheel...So take it up a notch. Dress louder. Start cursing more. Waste more time. You're making us look bad.

VII

Endless Desert

THERE WERE ARAB GROCERY STORES IN THE SOUTH SLOPE when I was little. You could call Arabs a lot of things, but never passive-aggressive. I don't think the Arabs have a word for "indirect." If you tried to steal, they'd come out from behind the counter and enforce the Code of Hammurabi right there.

All Mediterranean people are intimate, like the Italians, but Arabs are the most intense people on earth. You never hear an easygoing Middle Eastern proverb like "Different strokes for different folks" or "I'm okay, you're okay" or "Shiites are from Mars, Sunnis are from Venus."

Arabs will stare at you for an entire conversation until you are almost in a hypnotic state. If you talk to someone that committed for twenty minutes, then you're ready to drive a cement truck into the Wailing Wall.

Not big laughers, the Arabs. This makes stand-up difficult. That's why there are no Arab comedy clubs.

If you start a joke, "You ever notice when people do X?" and mention something annoying, you don't hear laughter. You hear stony silence, and then, "Why would you allow that impudence to go unpunished?"

"Hey, folks, ever notice how at the bank people cut in front of you on line?"

"Yes. When that happens, you stab them in the eye."

To resonate with the audience, the jokes need to be chilling:

A frog and a scorpion are sitting on the bank of the River Jordan. "Hey frog," says the scorpion. "I need to go to the other side of the river. Why don't you carry me across on your back?"

"Are you kidding?" says the frog. "You'll sting me."

"No I won't," says the scorpion. "If I stung you, we'd both drown."

"That's true," says the frog. "Hop on."

The scorpion climbs on the frog's back. Halfway across the Jordan River, the scorpion stings the frog.

"Why did you do that? Now we're both going to die" cries the frog, as they start to drown.

"Because this is the Middle East."

Like a lot of immigrant groups, New York City Arabs don't like to say no. They act like it's rude to say no. So they agree with you even if they don't. Arabs will answer your question by saying, "What do you want me to say?" "I want you to say how you feel!" I say. "What do you want that to be?" they reply.

But some Arabs do go against the grain, like the Christian Arabs. If there are people with bigger balls than the Navy SEALs, I'd say it's the people who live in the middle of Cairo and walk around with a cross around their neck. You think Madonna was edgy when *she* did it? Try walking down a street with a crucifix on your chest past eighty guys who just emptied out of a mosque. It's like wearing a Giants jersey into an Eagles bar.

* * *

Once I had an Iranian boss named Mohammad, who went by Mo. He was the manager of a restaurant where I worked, and he claimed to be a former close friend of the shah. He only drank Chivas Regal and always wore a suit. Like a lot of immigrants, he loved America and hated any trace of anti-Americanism. He thought complaining about the U.S. was an indulgence of spoiled Americans.

Mo was a lonely guy, all alone in the world save for hookers and bartenders and our restaurant staff, but I liked him, because he was a sarcastic bastard. He would take me to his favorite bar and buy me drinks. He was always impressed by anybody with an education. He was friendly but would talk behind everyone's back. When I went to the bathroom to do coke, he'd talk shit about me, and when somebody else at the bar went to the bathroom, he'd talk shit about them.

He was a generous man. He wouldn't let anyone pay for anything, so he had everyone in his pocket. Mo would bribe bar owners to stay open after hours and serve us. He'd pay anybody for anything, anytime. And like the shah's closest allies, those of us around him defended him for our own selfish reasons. We'd look the other way as he sexually harassed a waitress or was condescending to an inferior (like many immigrants, Mo believed fervently in the class system). He loved to get everyone drunk around him and then he'd yell quasi-sensical things like, "Oh boy! Mr. Taylor Mead I think don't like Mr. Jerzy Kosinski! I think maybe he's going to put you on the smelly bastard list! He thinks you are smelly bastard, and that's all, sir!"

I don't know if "smelly bastard" was an inside joke or if it was one of those things from childhood that only came out when he was drunk, like his father used to call him a "smelly bastard" and in his mind it was the worst possible insult.

When he got drunk he would also tell me crazy stories of Islamic radicals who stopped women in the streets and beat them up for wearing short skirts. At the time, I thought he was making it all up, but later I realized he was telling the truth. He was like a combination of Peter O'Toole and professional wrestler the Iron Sheik. He would start talking to girls at the bar, telling them, "Look at your legs, beautiful legs. You go to Iran, they wrap up legs." An aside: My aunt Margaret told me that when she wore her Catholic school uniform skirt too short, the nuns made her wrap toilet paper around her legs and walk like that from class to class. Not too traumatizing for a nine-year-old.

Iranians always say they're not Arabs, and we smile politely and think to ourselves, *Sure, you're not*, but at that time there were more Iranians like Mo, who really did seem like a very specific, non-Arab kind of Arab.

One night, Mo and I were drinking in a now long-gone bar in the Village, maybe the Cedar Tavern. And I'm telling these girls that I'm a writer working on a book about Brooklyn that's a direct response to *Saturday Night Fever*. "This one," I explained, "is a powerful Irish story set in Brooklyn that no one has ever told before." Never mind that I myself had already read about six by Pete Hamill. But I was very resentful that *Saturday Night Fever* had the temerity to publicize my borough without my making some profit off of it.

So I'm rambling, and then Mo picks up on the fact that I'm talking about Italians. He starts talking about when he was in Rome in 1965 with the shah and they gave a Czechoslovakian girl a hundred dollars to jump into the Trevi Fountain in her underwear or something. I don't remember the details, but I know it involved water, and something slightly illegal, and the purchase of another human being. Then Mo flirtatiously tells these girls he will give them fifty dollars if one of them sprays the bartender with the soda gun.

This bartender, by the way, hated me. Which you'll now surely recognize as a recurring theme. Even in my drunken stupor, I could tell the guy had no use for me. He saw me as a hanger-on and a loudmouth, and he resented the fact that I insisted on singing along every time a Rolling Stones song came on the jukebox. When "Beast of Burden" played, I cleverly changed the lyrics to "Pizza Server." No one ever laughed, but I figured maybe that was because they couldn't hear me, so I would sing-scream, "I'll never be…your… *PIZZA SERVER!*" at the top of my lungs. When they still didn't laugh, I figured that maybe it was just a visual crowd, and so I danced around chicken strutting and flapping my arms like Mick Jagger. When *that* didn't work, I smacked the jukebox to make it skip so I could yell "Pizza Server" over and over. You get the idea.

This bartender was always mean-mugging me, but he never let Mo see, because Mo was the greatest tipper who has ever lived. But the bartender was one of those people who, if there was ever a catastrophic disaster and all societal and social contracts disappeared into an orgy of violence and anarchy, would make a beeline for you with a machete and a blood-drenched smirk.

It turned out that the giggling girls didn't want to spray the bartender. I wanted the fifty bucks so I grabbed the soda sprayer and I did it myself. It soured the whole mood. The wet bartender was murderous. Mo was embarrassed and insulted—and Mo was a man who didn't like to be insulted. Sicilians and Albanians are famous for the lengths they will go to for revenge. The Iranians never forgive. And that was my cue to go into the bathroom to do more coke.

I go into the bathroom to take a piss and do a line.

During the coke days, the whole energy of a person or a night would swing wildly from minute to minute. People would go into the bathroom to do a line and come out with a murder plot against a friend that they left at the bar, for no reason other than they imagined some insult. But in this case it was the reverse. I came back to the bar happy as a lark.

Mo and the bartender were having a hushed conversation, and the bartender was on the phone. Mo saw me coming and said something to him, and he finished his call and hung up. Mo was being a little bit weird to me. He was acting normal, but his eyes had hate in them. They were lit up like De Niro in *Goodfellas* when "Sunshine of Your Love" is playing. And I just thought, *Fuck that, he's just mad about that fifty bucks.* I let it go.

The night breaks up and I leave and start walking on University when I notice a big guy in a doorway. "That guy looks like he's waiting to beat somebody's ass," I said to myself. Then he looks away from me and then back at me. And he had that look. He was kind of fat, but not living-with-Mom-and-playing-video-games fat, more like eating-Clemenza's-spaghetti-because-he's-gone-to-the-mattresses fat. We had that moment where we looked in each other's eyes and recognized what was going to happen. I started running around a car, with him chasing me, and neither of us said a word.

It was weird. I should've said, "Who sent you?" or "Who's your boss? I'll pay you double!" or something from

Kojak, but I knew I'd be running shortly, and as I was a heavy smoker I didn't want to waste any breath talking. He was holding something under his jacket. I was afraid it was a gun, but I was also afraid it was a pipe or tire iron, and I didn't want to be sitting there on a Village street with a head like a road map after this bastard opened my skull up. My only hope was the subway at Union Square, which in those days looked like something out of *The Walking Dead*. I ran faster than I've ever run, and I got away.

The next day at work I saw Mo. We never discussed the night before, but we also never went out together again. I could never prove it was Mo who sent the goon, and it may have been a weird coincidence or whatever, but all I'm saying is my takeaway was: Sicilians and Albanians will wait a hundred years for revenge, but Iranians won't wait an hour.

* * *

When I started at the Comedy Cellar in the late nineties, the guy who owned it was an Israeli named Manny (now his son owns it), and he had mostly Arab employees. You had Hassan (who went back to Egypt to open a McDonald's), Magdi, and Taweel (who's still there). We loved Hassan and Taweel. Anytime a fight broke out in the club, Hassan, a big guy, would come out of the kitchen waving a butcher knife. He had giant hands. He meant business. He came out not to scare people. He came out fully prepared to cut someone up.

Every night, Manny and the Arabs would fight about Israel. There'd be tables of people waiting for falafel while

Manny gave the cooks an earful about the Oslo accords. Hassan would accuse Mossad agents of turning Arab women into whores with aphrodisiac-laced chewing gum. They couldn't agree on anything.

Manny hired as manager Big John, an Italian-Irish guy who grew up in my neighborhood and became a Hells Angel. He had SS lightning-bolt tattoos, which initially freaked Manny out. But something told Manny to hire him, and he was right to do it. John was a reformed guy—one of those prison success stories—and brilliant, ahead of his time in computers. He died right after 9/11. I was one of the people who spoke at his funeral. The party afterward was the Israelis and Arabs from the Comedy Cellar, a bunch of comics, and the Hells Angels. It was an unlikely recipe for a great party, but for one day, we all got along like the best of friends.

* * *

Most of the New York Arabs are from Egypt and Yemen. Egypt's problem is that it's the exotic girl who got old. Cleopatra is still wearing too much eye makeup. It looks hot when you're young, but when you're over two thousand you look like Dame Edna. Egypt is trying to bring back the empire, but their empire was all about tombs and graves. The Egyptians went from building pyramids to harassing women in Tahrir Square. New York Egyptians are considered the humorous Arabs, which I understand is like being the charismatic Canadians.

Yemenis ran a lot of delis in New York, and the ones I've talked to say the meanest things about Egyptians, like: "They think they're funny." When everyone's dividing up countries, nobody yells, "Yo, I got Yemen!" Nobody wants Yemen, trust me. If we are the world's policeman, Yemen's the house that when you get the call you go, "Oh shit. Not there." It's like gang territory. Everybody in Yemen just stares at the cars going by, waiting for someone to be unlucky enough to break down there.

I never saw many Saudi Arabians in New York, but maybe that's because I wasn't a bellhop at the Sherry-Netherland ushering them, five prostitutes, and two off-duty NYPD through the back entrance up to the penthouse. Saudi Arabia is the rich girl that the other girls don't like but they tolerate her because she buys them things. She buys her friends. But behind her back they all talk about her. "Who's that bitch think she is, acting snooty? Sucking America's dick like the ho that she is?"

Have you ever seen press interviews with the children of Saudi royalty? They always have two sons—one devout and one lascivious. The first is on message with the rage and the conservatism: "The woman must stay in the kitchen, cooking!" But the second is suave. "I will admit my country is not perfect," he says. "For one thing, you can't get a decent cappuccino. Am I right?" He's telling Richard Engel things like, "You must come hunting with us. I bagged a hundred-year-old turtle last year." The first brother is saying, "Down with America! Down with the Jews!" while the other one is off camera, whispering to Christiane Amanpour, "I want to drink champagne out of your Spanx. I want to eat your pussy on a Jet Ski in the Gulf of Aden."

When I was growing up, the Syrians lived in Bay Ridge, Brooklyn, and everyone called pita bread "Syrian bread." Syria has been in a state of emergency since 1963. That's more than fifty years. You have to be a good bullshit artist to pull that off.

"What's up? Is it safe yet?"

"Not yet. But it's only been seventeen years. Just a few more weeks, maybe a month. We'll let you know... Almost... Almost."

Syria has no oil, but it's friends with guys that have oil. That's how the Mideast is. The countries without the oil hate on anybody who's not nice to the countries that have the oil. If you're trying to get with some girl, you know you have to be nice to her friends even if you hate them, or else they will destroy you to her.

Turkey gets away with everything. Nobody ever criticizes them. They committed genocide but everyone says, "Eh, that was a long time ago." We try to say, "Hey, Turkey, go easy on those Kurds, okay?" But then we see those crazy green eyes, and we're like, "Never mind." Or we're like, "Hey, you're not dealing drugs, right? Because some people are saying... Who? It doesn't matter who. Right, they're full of shit. For sure."

They are the guy that, any time he gets in a fight, it's so ugly that nobody wants to mess with him ever again. He lives in kind of a tough neighborhood, and you notice when he walks down the block no one looks him in the eye.

* * *

Ten years ago, I was banned from Afghanistan. You can't do worse in this era than to be banned from there. Drug mules, traffickers, mercenaries, warlords, mujahideen, bin Laden in the nineties—all acceptable. Colin Quinn—not welcome.

I guess I made one fatal joke about all the sodomy there between mullahs and teenage boys. The Taliban wear mascara and color their beards. Big military guys wearing Linda Evangelista eye makeup are staring down teenage boys. "The commander finds you to be a delightful person," they say. I said nothing that's not in *The Kite Runner*. For a place that hates gay people so much, there's an awful lot of activity going on behind those rusted Russian tanks.

"What do you do if you find a gay guy—kill him?" I asked this guy I met on my Middle Eastern travels.

"If he act and dress like woman, that good," he said. "But if he act like a man, and you find out he do it, then you kill him." I guess they like to know what they're getting.

How could I be on a stage in Afghanistan and not mention the local flavor? It's impossible to suppress those things. When I did a gig at Disney once, right before I went onstage they said, "Don't make jokes about Disney." The second I got up there I started making fun of cold, dead Walt.

Something just happens to you when you're told not to do something. You can't help it. Someone tells you, "Don't talk about the guy in the blue shirt. He runs this city." You nod, but the second you're up there, you hear yourself say to the evil town boss, "Hey, guy in the blue shirt! You look like Ben Gazzara in *Road House*."

Comedians are reality checks for everyone. That's why we also have a moral obligation to take down hecklers.

Sometimes, they're just drunk fans interrupting your show with "I love you, man!" Or turning to their boyfriends and saying, loudly, after every bit, "Oh my God! That happened to me last week! Remember when we did that? It's so true!" But the ones you really have to destroy are the guys who think they're comedians but who nobody paid to see. They're always the douche in a group of two or four. What you do is you stay calm and figure a way to ruin them.

Nick DiPaolo doesn't hesitate. He just goes right into taking the guy down, as if it's an expected part of his day that's finally arrived. Patrice O'Neal always took the long way around and then brought shame down on the guy like a tidal wave. I go for the psychological exam: Look at who they're with, figure out the bigger picture, and then try to hit them where Freud would.

A censor, like a heckler, comes to symbolize every asshole the audience works with, and every other bully. They're trying to usurp the power that you hold because you have the microphone. That's why in Afghanistan I got onstage and immediately started talking about sodomy.

* * *

I was at LaGuardia Airport soon after 9/11. The TSA officer checking my bag through was wearing a hijab and she was reading a book called *Women and Fatwa in Islam*. I did a show that week and mentioned that incident. In the audience, someone said, "That's Islamophobic." If I see a priest reading a magazine with One Direction on the cover, and I make a joke about it, yes, that priest, who's probably just reading *Tiger Beat* for the articles, is being judged based on the actions of a few of his frisky colleagues.

In 2002, I got my own show, Comedy Central's *Tough Crowd with Colin Quinn*, and we talked about race a lot, especially the race in the news so much during this period: the Arabs. Before 9/11, you just were like, "Oh, this guy, I guess he's Arab." After 9/11, you see a story in the news about a predator drone attack and both you and the Arabs are looking at each other out of the corner of your eyes. Only the Jews noticed the Arabs were Arabs before 9/11. The Arabs think everybody is Jewish—you know how many Arab cabbies have been arguing politics with me and suddenly they stop and ask, "Are you Jewish?"

I loved doing *Tough Crowd*. It ran in what became the *Colbert Report* time slot. Colbert did okay with that slot, too—whatever. Anyway, it was a stressful time in the wake of September 11, and the guests and I kept the mood light by ruining one another's day.

Like once, Jim Norton showed up at the taping complaining. He kept talking and talking and talking. He was berating me for something. And the whole time, he was holding his cherished, perfectly made coffee from Starbucks, a twenty-minute walk from our middle-of-nowhere studio. There were no other coffee options for blocks.

On this day, he had waited in a long line and given a complicated order. He'd paid several dollars. He'd invested a solid half hour and a lot of hopes and dreams in that coffee. I was eating a sandwich. Just as Norton reached the crescendo of yelling at me, I calmly broke off a piece of my roast beef and dropped it in his coffee. The coffee was ruined. Jim was speechless. I'll remember his Mongoloid frown, and smile on my deathbed.

I feel like that show was my career downfall. We were an ethnically diverse bunch of guys talking honestly about race. A lot of it was not politically correct. Every day was a black-white fight. And a rough-and-tumble conversation about Islam, too. To put it mildly, that was really not in keeping with the zeitgeist. Somehow I acquired this conservative label—never mind that I've been a registered Democrat for decades. A lot of lip service gets paid to being honest, but no one really wants to hear it unless what's being said is the party line.

Nick DiPaolo was one of the hardest to make laugh and one of the quickest to anger. He goes from zero to sixty like the Arabs I'm supposed to be talking about right now. I would amuse myself by playing the same prank, which he actually fell victim to for several years running. Here's how it goes:

Colin Quinn

I am flipping channels and come across a delightful rom-com. I will let *When Harry Met Sally* slide, because everyone loves it and you can't pick a fight with the entire world. Let's say *City Slickers II*, one of the most horrible things I've ever encountered. And yet, when it's on TV, I can't look away. I have seen it five or six times.

Okay, so you have the terrible movie on. *You've Got Mail* works, as does *My Life in Ruins*. Any family-friendly romantic nightmare movie is good. Then you call Nick.

"Hey, Nick, what's up?" you say.

"What?" he snaps, surly bastard that he is.

"Well, I'm just flipping channels."

[Blah, blah, pretend you're listening to whatever he's saying, make small talk.]

"Oh shit!" you say. "Turn on HBO! They have this thing on right now—it's about the Boston Bruins' all-time best fights!"

[Pause while he finds his remote and runs to the TV and turns it on and...sees Billy Crystal in Western wear, nuzzling a baby cow.]

Silence. And then: "Fuck you, Colin."

* * *

On *Tough Crowd*, my producer would always be bringing me footage of these imams who were stirring up so much hatred against the United States. I started to see what they really are: the stand-up comics/motivational speakers of the

182

terrorist world. The popular ones began by making jokes about Western decadence and infidels being spoiled. Then they yelled at the crowd:

"You don't think Muhammad got tired when he was fighting to reclaim Mecca? You think Saladin said, 'Oh, those crusaders! I think I am going to sit this one out. The Belgians are too tough; they might hit me with some waffles'? Well, that's what you are doing! Waffling. I can't wait to see when you get to paradise. There will be no seventy-two virgins for you, my friends—maybe six chicks with bad perms and dirty fingernails. Eternity for you will be a bad dance sponsored by a singles website. You will be standing around with a Shasta Cola and a fistful of potato chips listening to Ace of Base. And then you can say, 'I saw the sign, but I *didn't* open up my eyes,' you lonely, uncomfortable, wallflower, half-committed pieces of shit."

Why do we fight suicide bombers with troops on the ground? Fight fire with fire. We should send our people who are already suicidal. We could say, "That's terrible. You shouldn't kill yourself. But if you really feel you have to, can you drop off this package first?" And see how they do.

* * *

Leaders in some of these countries behave like your drunk friend who acts belligerent, starts fights with everyone, runs up tabs, and somehow you're the one who ends up in jail, or getting beaten up, or going broke. His big mouth gets your ass kicked. And at the end of the night, he's nowhere to be found. Then you call him the next day. "Hey, where are you?" And he says, "In Paris, brother."

That's the kind of shit we have to deal with as the world's policeman. We started out idealistic, to protect and serve the world. Now we're overweight and just hoping to not lose our pension.

Us [*pulling up to Afghanistan*]: "What do we got here?"

OTHER COP (THE U.K.): "This guy claims that since the fourth century these guys have been messing with him, raiding his villages. Plundering the wealth."

Us: "Good evening, sir. I hear you're a Communist. I hear you harbor terrorists. Can I see your ID, please? You harbor terrorists? Is that what you do?"

THEM: "That's Turkmenistan. Come on, you guys always think I'm Azerbaijan. We all look alike, is that it?"

Us: "What you got in the saddlebags?"

THEM: "That's not even my donkey, bro. I never seen that thing before."

Us: "Look, I want to go easy on you, but my partner, Great Britain here, wants to impose sanctions..."

The Coloring Book

We have a strange relationship with other countries. We tell them, "Fight! We have your back." They fight. Then we forget about them because we are busy dealing with another country.

And everybody hates us. We're always bragging: "We're the greatest! We're the richest!" When you say stuff like that, people go, "If you're the greatest and richest, help us!" You don't hear China saying that. They keep their mouth shut.

* * *

I've been to Iraq a few times on USO tours. The first time I sliced into that sand trap was in 2003. I made that trip with my assistant—a perky Louisiana hayseed named Ellen— and the comics Jim Norton and Laurie Kilmartin. Laurie has since married a very cute young Mexican comic. I hear now that he's gotten the *carta*, he's splayed out on the air mattress in the master bedroom/extended Silverado cab analyzing wrestling magazines like they're the Talmud and yelling in Spanglish for another *cerveza fría*, while the once-proud quasi-feminist uses her copy of *The Beauty Myth* as a changing table for her triplets. But that's her journey, as they say.

But let's get to the other fellow traveler on the Iraq journey, one James "Mommy, why does that man have a cascading neck?" Norton. It was my tour, and like a magnanimous Sunni chieftain I was kind enough to bring Jim along. He came cheap. His dressing room rider included:

wood chips instead of a rug, a giant wheel for exercise, and pellet food.

The first few shows went off without a hitch. Then we hit New Year's Eve. We're in the tent getting ready for the big show at one of Saddam's palaces, when the USO representative, Tracy, informs us that, due to possible danger from incoming insurgent fire, the show might have to be canceled.

Of course, I took this news with the grace and low-key humility that I've worked tirelessly to display. So everything is fine. Laurie is cool. Ellen is cool. Tracy is cool. I'm cool. But then suddenly I hear a quiet buzzing in the tent.

At first I thought it was one of the giant flying insects that have been flying around this part of the world since the Old Testament. I looked around for a newspaper to put a stop to it, when suddenly we all looked and realized it wasn't an insect—at least not in the conventional sense. No, it was Jim muttering to himself and walking spastically around the room in circles waiting for someone to notice him and ask what was the problem.

Tracy or Ellen inquired and Jim, with a look of sullen reproach on his idiotic baby face, blurts out, "I've been doing comedy for twelve years, and I've never missed a New Year's show." He sulks dramatically; the rest of us stand in stunned silence.

Let me state the situation one more time. We were in Iraq. In a war zone. There are boys and girls putting their young bodies in harm's way every day to defend our barely defensible way of life here in the United States. They're not getting a lot of high-profile celebrity visits. (I know that you knew that from the fact that we were there.) But the celebrities that do visit at least give these brave youngsters the reassurance that people appreciate the sacrificial nature of what they are trying to do.

In the midst of that, this incubated hatchling is strutting around, quacking, feathers ruffling, because people don't realize that this trip is not about giving brief respite to the nineteen-year-olds seeing the frontline horrors and depravities that will never leave their minds. No, no, no, no, no. That's important, sure. But more pressing is keeping the torch lit on the unnoticed and immaterial New Year's record of this ludicrous goblin.

I bet our troops would have doubled their valor and courage if they knew that they were protecting the right of a drone to live in a movie within his own mind—a movie in which twelve December 31s in various New Jersey townships drinking a post-show glass of cream soda while being treated to a perfunctory suck-off by a bewildered blubber bunny trying not to smear her hair glitter matter at all, to anyone.

That's why we could never win in Iraq, because we're all under the impression that our way of life is precious. Even a guy like Jim Norton is clinging to his one empty tradition like anyone gives a care. My prayers for his death, as always, went unanswered.

* * *

Arabs have a far-reaching sense of their history. One might even say too far. Everybody has to be related to Muhammad. No Christian tries to trace their family back to Jesus. You never hear, "Turns out my uncle was the Virgin Mary's great-grandson and his father was the one that introduced Joseph and Mary because he worked with Joseph. He was on the list but Nazareth was impossible to break into. Back in those days you had to go to Arimathea..."

There's a lot of hand-wringing about who should have Jerusalem—Christians, Muslims, or Jews. But Muslims, you've got Mecca and Medina, so why don't you let us have this one? It's your third choice! You don't even care about it that much. Let the Christians and those other people (I don't want to get you riled up by mentioning their name) have it. But it's like you got into your first two college choices, Harvard and Yale, and we got into our first choice, Princeton, and now you're trying to take our place in Princeton. You give us Jerusalem and we'll stop making cartoons.

Arabs, you're a passionate people, but you're too much. Calm down; you're going to have a heart attack. That thousand-yard stare of yours is a bit disconcerting. Blink once in a while to let us know everything's alright. I know most of you don't agree with extremists. But if there's someone in the room right now and you can't talk, signal me by standing at the window with a rose and a copy of *The Feminine Mystique*.

VIII

Blood Blue

In the late 1990s, you actually started to see white people in New York. Overnight, it became more Anglo-Saxon and Protestant. TV shows like *Sex and the City* and *Friends* convinced suburban kids that New York would be a fun place to be, and so they moved to the city and taught all the bartenders how to make appletinis.

At that time, I was on *Saturday Night Live*, one of the few comedy scenes on earth with almost no Jews. Lorne Michaels is Jewish, but he's also Canadian, so that cancels out his Jewishness and makes him an honorary WASP. The WASPs are more or less a mythical race at this point, but it is true that white people who don't scan as Italian, Jewish, or Irish have been in the past thirty years taking over New York.

The real WASPs who barely exist anymore, they

perfected a certain way of life—the lawns, the furniture, the clothes, the etiquette. The sweater around the neck. Think about how cocky that is. A sweater is there to keep you from freezing to death or to hide your physical imperfections. And these people are wearing them around their necks. And they're always wearing white. Everybody else is trying to hide the wear and tear on their clothes by wearing dark colors. The WASPs are saying, "We don't have stains because we have perfect table manners so we don't spill anything on our clothes." They drove everybody crazy with their boats, houses, and naming the kids Chet and Jacqueline. Because of the WASPs, all immigrants came here thinking *I'll shit in a bucket and live in a tenement but my grandkids are going to have piano lessons and tennis rackets and trust funds.*

WASPs are still pretty dominant in New England, though up there they've now got a whole Portuguese-Brazilian thing going on since the past couple of centuries, because of the fishing and the seafaring activities. The Portuguese make great seafood stew, and I heard they've been known to be around the Ironbound section of Newark, and that's all I got. It's their own fault for being vague. I don't know what to say about New England. Those people don't really come down below Mystic, Connecticut, much, so it's hard for me to gather my thoughts on such matters.

But I do know that in New York, the WASP is generally considered the bad guy. In movies and on TV shows, they're always wrong, the go-to villain. Once I went on a *Law & Order* kick and watched sixty episodes over the course of a couple of weeks. Do you know how many of the criminals portrayed on the show were not white? Three. Apparently most violent crime in New York City is committed at the elite Dalton School. I find it hard to believe that non-white people make up 55 percent of the population of New York City but are responsible for only 5 percent of the TV crime. That's not even the percentage in Finland. If they had their way, TV and movie execs would produce a history of the Crips starring Greg Kinnear.

There is a serious strain of white self-hatred in our culture right now. From Opus Dei in Catholicism to the Shia, self-flagellation has been used to purify for many years. And for the last thirty years or so, white people have been trying to solve the race issue by taking all the sins of the world on their shoulders. That's why all villains in our movies are either hillbillies, blonde sorority and fraternity types, or portly, balding white businessmen.

And are the WASPs of today really such bad guys in real life? Truth be told, when the WASPs ran Wall Street they robbed correctly. It's when the Irish, Italians, and Jews ran it and got greedy and tried to act like WASPs that they tanked it. They were strivers and went crazy. The Irish were more or less the new WASPs, starting with the Kennedys. Jews and Italians admire WASPs. They want to go skiing to be more like them. But they're into it sort of like how Rodney Dangerfield was into the stuff Ted Knight had in *Caddyshack*. People built skyscrapers and invented technology and traded derivatives and robbed pensions and all so that they could feel that feeling of sitting down in an enclosed porch in a room full of books in an old Colonial in Cos Cob, Connecticut, and have a glass of port.

As the rest of America moved into New York, a lot of old-time New York left. The dirtbags moved to the suburbs, and all the suburbanites moved to the city. They moved there for diversity, but they brought their blandness with them. Luckily, they also brought frozen yogurt, which is delicious.

In my building, suddenly all these people came in with a lot of outdoor sporting equipment. They went to the park. They rode bikes and even wore helmets. The level of enthusiasm became intolerable. But looking at them, you see why this country was built successfully—WASPs are chore-oriented. When they came to New York, there were ten times as many hardware stores. That's how America was built: boring, task-oriented, white people saying, "We need another sheet of quarter-inch plywood."

Even at *Saturday Night Live*, people said, "What are you doing Sunday? We're going to the museum!"

I was like, *What?* Museums are for class trips when you're eight. Only Jewish people go to museums after that point. Otherwise, for us, they were all just directions, signposts where to go. "Make a right at that museum of rare buttons on the corner."

New York City's gentrification process is basically some poor people move into a neighborhood, then hipsters, then bankers. The Italian neighborhoods were easy to take over. The landlords said, "Give me $50K, I'll move to Staten

Island, no problem." The Hasidic neighborhoods were hard: "Fifty years ago, Avram sold that building on Roebling. Now there's a beer pong bar there. Our people will never sell a building again."

But eventually, always, the hipsters infiltrate, and the bankers follow them. And then the hipsters move out and find a new neighborhood and the bankers follow them there, and so on. That's the actual definition of gentrification: the bankers chasing the hipsters all over the city.

This happened in the East Village, then Williamsburg, then Bushwick. One reason WASPy people are successful in conquering New York neighborhoods is that the hipsters pave the way for them, but another reason is that WASPs are so friendly and well intentioned.

When Bedford-Stuyvesant, stomping ground to Jay Z and Biggie, started sprouting bistros, that surprised even me. Black people there were so used to white people moving away from them that when they saw these white people coming into their buildings with a big smile and a bunch of art and hardware supplies, they didn't know how to react.

Locals are ready to hate the newcomers, but then here come these cheerful white people, so chipper: "Hello there, neighbor!" That's the one weapon that not even the toughest community in New York City was prepared to combat: affability. Guns, knives, bats, but the one thing they never thought you'd get hit with is a can-do attitude. How can you argue with the energy that built the West?

Suddenly, the longtime black residents are standing

there, holding a plate of brownies, stunned, saying, "Did you know the wood molding in my house dates back to the 1920s? These white people are going to help me strip the paint on it. And they agree with everything I say."

These new white people hate the white man, too. They've been to liberal arts colleges where they learned about oppression and condemn it. And so there they are, these people who look like they stepped out of a Norman Rockwell painting, on the sidewalks of Bed-Stuy, singing along with Notorious B.I.G.'s "Ten Crack Commandments," sanding chairs.

* * *

Cities used to be dangerous. Now some are clean and landscaped and have an outdoor mall with a not-real name like the Promenade, or the Citiwalk, or the Riverwalk. It used to be that the city was hard and the suburbs were soft. Now it's the other way around. Chicago used to have a ton of Eastern Europeans: Polish, Turks, and Slavs. That goes back to the days of meatpacking, because they all only need three hours of sleep and have those thick fingers that can dig into a side of beef and throw it over their shoulder. Of course, that was before the Haymarket Square Riot of 1886. Now the slaughterhouses are all lofts and the stockyards have been converted into an outdoor entertainment and dining complex with a Dave & Buster's and a comedy club and a Ballocity ball room and a climbing wall and a free-fall ride and a laser tag maze and buses full of bachelorette parties.

New York's been cleaned up, too. Nobody wants to give

Giuliani credit for cleaning up New York City in the 1990s. But c'mon. This was a guy who took down the mob, even closing the Fulton Fish Market. That was more symbolic than all the other mob businesses put together. I remember when that closed, people were like, "Oh my God, they're going to kill him!" But he lived. Under him, John Gotti's social club was replaced by a designer's studio.

Meanwhile, the suburbs have become terrifying. Last time I was in West Palm Beach, the CityPlace was like the new East New York. You go there at six at night and there are street performers with knife scars. The photo booth says, "Take a picture with an AK-47." The stuffed-animal prizes are wearing Kevlar. A few years back, they robbed David Copperfield in West Palm Beach, for chrissake. Yes, it's funny: "Yo, empty your pockets," and he pulls out a bunny rabbit. But if someone who can make himself disappear isn't safe, who is?

* * *

I never thought I'd see the day when the ethnic group running New York was the nerds. The thug thing is gone, and inner-city kids are wearing Buddy Holly glasses. It's because we need smart people to deal with the Martian invasion or whatever's coming down the pike at us. We need people who can operate lasers and Hadron colliders.

Hipsters are an offshoot of nerds. When the nerds took power with computers, hipsters said, "We're socially awkward, because it's cool." The hipsters took their place as

nerds-with-self-esteem. The first hipsters were Weezer—
they started as nerds and ended as hipsters.

Since the nineties, black and white culture have split in
two: white singers wearing old clothes and saying, "I'm a
loser, baby," and black singers wearing diamonds and saying, "We're going global! Tony Montana style!" Can you
imagine them reversed? Some twee band like Belle and
Sebastian popping corks on yachts and Kanye saying, "I
mean, I'm doing okay. I'm not the *best* or anything. What
is success, really? Want to try these pickles I made?"

* * *

As a Brooklyn kid, on Saturday afternoons I walked over to
the record store at Fifth Avenue and 5th Street to buy 45s.
It was dangerous, but I couldn't resist going down there to
get my fix of all the hot new jams. Once there, you had five
minutes to leave the block at a healthy clip before you'd
be descended on for the simple crime of not living there.
You could walk on any block, but you couldn't stop. The
only signal you had that your time was up was an old lady
would suddenly leave her window and shut it, and that's
when you were dead. That's when it was too late. I've read
that Tommy from Tommy James and the Shondells had a
rough life and claimed the Mafia stole all his money. Well, I
hope he appreciated the fact that he wasn't the only one who
had it hard; I literally put my life at risk to buy his goddamn
song "I Think We're Alone Now."

Now my old neighborhood looks like Darien, Connecticut. Back in the day, if someone asked, "Where are you from?" and you said, "Brooklyn," you'd get instant street cred, as if you'd spent all day rumbling with the Baseball Furies. Now it's a smirk and, "Really?" as if you've spent all day baking artisanal gluten-free scones—which, if you live in Brooklyn today, you probably have.

Yes, NYC in the seventies was psychotic. People would go to a Broadway show and then bolt for the parking lot. No one got on the subway, and no one strolled. It's easier to glorify the *Taxi Driver* days if you're a French film student than if you actually lived through them.

But the city threw the baby out with the bathwater. Like I said, Giuliani cleaned up the city, but he kept scrubbing even after it was already clean. I think he has OCD. Now you see all these naturally blond people running everywhere. The L train to Brooklyn looks like a ski lift. When I walk through Times Square, even though it's safer, it looks like Harajuku Disneyland. It's all Europeans wandering around Manhattan with their giant cameras. It's like the Dutch have returned to New York after four hundred years and are reminding us that they used to be in charge by blocking the subway doors.

Every culture has its elephants in the room. New York's is gentrification. In India, there are literally elephants in some rooms. "Really, there's an elephant in the corner. Let's get him out of here." Our country was created by WASPs—the founding fathers. Yes, they were slaveholders, but they also wrote the Constitution. Look at Phil Spector: Sure, he's a murderer, but "Be My Baby" is a pretty good song. Do I feel creepy watching *Annie Hall* knowing about Woody Allen's personal life? Of course. And I get that's how black people feel about the WASPs who wrote the Constitution.

* * *

From the *Mayflower* to the bank bailout, WASPs benefited the most from this country, and so it's them who everybody envies and hates. Being of "English" stock, you had to know that it was only a matter of time before everybody turned on you. After all, the whole idea was to get away from England and the class system, and, for better and for worse, you've always seemed to be a class above everybody else. And as each group of immigrants came along they had to work for you, and they held on to their resentment even as they succeeded. Even as the polo ponies and the tennis courts and East Hampton became less and less WASPy, and you started to get an inferiority complex—I notice you now spend most of your time apologetically downplaying your family name and watching portrayals of your alcoholic, eccentric family secrets in Off-Broadway plays—you still embody the ideal that everyone aspires to.

Even with the infidelity and the unhappiness and the hypocrisy, you made that life look damn good. You were the ones who actualized the American Dream and made us want to wrest it from your cold, dead hands.

IX

Ellis Island Indigo

A CENTURY AGO, IMMIGRANTS FLOODED TO THESE SHORES. They moved into crowded tenements on the Lower East Side, and greedy landlords exploited them. It was unsterile and noisy, so they worked to get out. Their children finally got nicer apartments in the Bronx, but they were still tenements and it was still noisy and unsanitary, so they worked to get out. The grandkids finally moved out to the suburbs to raise their kids—who hated the suburbs because they were too quiet and sterile. So the great-grandkids moved back to the Lower East Side and Brooklyn and lived six people to a tenement, and the greedy landlords exploited them.

If you want to talk about immigration in the last twenty years, the entire story is right there on the 7 train. If you see a guy reading the *Irish Echo* or a Tagalog paper, those are Irish or Filipinos. They'll be getting off at 46th in Sunnyside. If someone's reading Hindi, they'll hop off at 74th in Jackson Heights. If somebody's reading Spanish and they look dolled up, they'll be sashaying off at 82nd, because they're Colombian. But if they're reading a Spanish paper and wearing construction gear, they're getting off at 103rd in Corona, because they're Mexican. If they're reading a Chinese newspaper, they're not getting off until the last stop, Flushing Main Street.

All immigrants make fun of us behind our backs. They go home and say, "I need a vacation, I worked two days in a row, I am American!" They think we are ungrateful and complaining, but they don't get it. That's what you do when things go well. Over here we're looking for career fulfillment. They're looking for stomach fulfillment.

And all the immigrants that come over here are pretty hard-core. Every group has to pay off their smugglers, their relatives, their community leaders. They manage to send a couple of bucks home and they have to try to learn English. Not easy. Meanwhile, every time I go to Canada, I have to keep asking, "Is this a dollar or a quarter?"

* * *

An honorable mention goes to the following ethnicities, who would be insulted if they weren't included. Your sections are short, but you are undiminished. It's your fault that you either moved here after 1990 or lived off a train like the J, which nobody ever takes.

GREEKS

Greeks invented critical thinking. They were original thinkers, but now they're going to take everybody down with them. "Hey, we invented half the shit the world uses and now you want to tell us we're broke?" We invented theater and democracy and sports and yet we don't get any royalties.

Greeks owned all the diners in Park Slope when I was young. Why? Because they're the masters of rude/polite. They're welcoming you warmly and seating you and at the same time they are rushing you out the door. "Hello, welcome my friend, get the guy coffee, you want coffee right, you hungry—eggs? How you like them? Scrambled? What kind of toast? Get the guys eggs with toast and throw some bacon on there. Where's the coffee? Sit down. Give him the check. Pay right up front. No problem. Come back soon, okay?"

RUSSIANS

The Russians moved into Brighton Beach and I remember my girlfriend Gwenn complaining about how they took her laundry out of the dryer in her building before it was dry. I thought, *She's imagining it*, but those early Russians were like that. They were pushy. They had come right out of Communism, where it was a dog-eat-dog existence, and they couldn't shake that elbow-you-under-the-boards mentality. Russians are still rude, but the accent gives them a lot of leeway. It's why people from Ireland can call you a cunt and you think it's charming. Russians are very jaded. That's another true cliché. Whenever they run into some positive American who tries to cheer them up and put them in a good mood, I can see them thinking, *What's wrong with this idiot?*

They are very critical and they have no filter. If you bore them, they tell you you're boring. I was hanging out with a Russian girl back in the early eighties when I was bartending, and she told me I was no fun. Do you know how not fun you have to be for that to happen? And don't try to cheer them up. Cheerful Russians would be like somber Australians. They are not chirpy people. They don't revere enthusiasm and positivity the way we do. You can't really imagine a Russian soccer mom dancing in the audience at Ellen.

ALBANIANS

If you're trying to figure out where someone who seems white is from, call him Russian; if he laughs, he's Greek, and if he says, "Call me Russian again and I'll cut your throat," then he's Albanian.

Fordham Road in the Bronx was filled with Albanians in the eighties. They were black-eyed badasses in disco clothes who would take it all the way every time. It quickly became apparent to everybody that if you wanted to start a fight with an Albanian, it would become a lifelong commitment. There's no expression "Forgive and forget" in Albania. There weren't many of them in New York. They were like modern-day Spartans—*300* is really a documentary about a group of Albanians fighting the rest of the Bronx. You know how they tell couples "Don't go to bed angry." Well, I'm telling you, don't leave the Bronx until you're sure that some Albanian isn't holding a grudge.

That lack of fear makes Albanians the scariest people on earth. Ask Liam Neeson. They casually memorize your face so they can remember to kill you if you ever disrespect them in the future. And everything is disrespectful to the Albanians. If you laugh when they are saying something: dead. If you wave at the smoke when they light up a cigarette in the car: dead. If you say something positive about the Serbians: dead.

GERMANS

There are three blocks of Germans left in Ridgewood, all sweeping their stoops like synchronized swimmers. When I was a kid, there was a German baker on my block. All of us little imps would run there and sing, "Whistle while you work; Hitler is a jerk. Mussolini bit his peenie, now it doesn't work! Heil Hitler!" and run out.

The Berlin Wall may have come down, but a divide remains: West Germany works hard, while East Germany is used to the government taking care of it. West Germany comes home from work like, "Did you even look for a job today, East Germany?" And East Germany's like, "Yeah, I called a few places. It's tough out there right now." And West Germany looks in the fridge and says, "Did you eat all the bratwurst?" And East Germany's like, "Did you want me to starve?"

Why did the German empire fall? The Russian invasion. They went into Russia. It's like going into your depressed friend's apartment on a nice day trying to get him out and about. You suggest a trip to the beach. An hour later there you are, sitting with him in a room with sunlight struggling to peek through the closed venetian blinds, watching TV and eating shitty food.

EASTERN EUROPEANS

A lot of people say that Eastern Europeans are miserable because of Communism. But that's not true. Communism is blameless here. These people have always been miserable from day one. Communism didn't exactly cheer up the Eastern Europeans, but Eastern Europe wasn't exactly Palm Beach when it arrived.

The basic problem with these societies is that they don't really have any natural resources. Their main products are barbells and doorknockers (not earrings, *mami*, but actual doorknockers that are made of steel but are shaped like lions or demons. The ones that you knock on the door and then an old guy comes out and says, "*Yeeesss*? Can I *heeeeelllp yooou*?").

Eastern Europe is full of maniacs. Then you combine that with weird clothes and language that sounds like they need to quit dairy, and what do you have? They are good-looking, I will give them that. But then once they're past forty-five they look like trolls or monsters and they all grow moles that look like wild mushrooms.

Serbia and Croatia and all those countries in the Balkans hate each other because they're all crammed together. The more accessible someone is, the less you appreciate them. It's like how you can come see me do comedy for the price of a drink at a bar in New York and so you don't respect me as much as the ever-mysterious Bradley Cooper. That's what I—and these constantly warring little countries smashed up against each other—get for being too available: disrespect.

Next to the Balkans are the Romanians. They are mostly gypsies. Gypsy men walk around breaking things and then charging people to fix them. Their wives charge lonely girls fifty dollars to look into an emptied-out snow globe and predict they'll meet a guy next year if they go on an *Eat, Pray, Love* trip.

Bulgarians are the weight lifters. They flex by the Black Sea. They are strong, but a little fat, too. They remind me of heavyweight UFC fighters who go around bumping people out of the way. Like the kid who always has to say something smart and then bumps you and barely says excuse me. "Yo, excuse you!" That's what I would say to Bulgaria. The Bulgarians just stand there while their hot girlfriends stroke the guys' hairy backs. They get sunburned except wherever their bling is.

Hungary is conceited, because it used to be a big deal. I'm still not sure why. Maybe because they invented peasant blouses? But then the 1920 Treaty of Trianon hit them after World War I. Oh my God, they got hammered. They walked out of that room like, "Yo, use Vaseline next time!" They had to give away everything and pay everybody. That's when they put a curse on all the Allies: France, England, us. World War II came about because of a Hungarian curse. Hungarians invented voodoo. They were known as the "White Haitians" back in the day. Anytime you needed somebody to get bad luck, you went to Hungary with a picture of the asshole and the Hungarians took it from there. Next thing you know, your enemy is walking around scratching because he has fleas or lost his job or his cat died. It sounds crazy, but it works. That's how the Hungarians got real estate on the Upper East Side.

Everybody makes jokes about how stupid the Polish are. But they came up with the helicopter, so that's impressive. Then the first pilot died because he got cold so he turned off the fan. But that could happen to anybody. Then they lost the war because the Germans marched in backward and so they thought they were leaving. But it's a new Poland now. In fact, I was recently at a lovely party in Greenpoint, the famous Polish neighborhood in Brooklyn. I hope it doesn't fall below sea level or they'll have to break out the old submarine with a screen door.

SCANDINAVIANS

Robert Moses chased all the blond Scandinavian families out of Brooklyn by dropping the Brooklyn-Queens Expressway in the middle of everything. He's the reason there were no 6' Norwegian supermodels walking through Brooklyn (until the last five years). The Scandinavians fled and left that part of Brooklyn to the hookers and drunks. So I didn't grow up around many Nordic people. But I did have a Norwegian uncle who during World War II was captured by the Germans. The German commander reading the list of prisoners' names got to my uncle.

"Lilja?" he said. "What's a nice Norwegian boy like you doing fighting on the wrong side?"

When the prisoner-of-war camps were liberated, my poor uncle, a nineteen-year-old kid, weighed ninety-nine pounds. General George Patton was making a tour of the liberated camps and someone asked him, "Do you want to meet with the POWs?" And he said, "No, I don't talk to cowards. They should have died before they let themselves be taken." My uncle hated Patton until he died.

The Vikings thought they were big shots because they had boats. You know how obnoxious people get when they own a boat. They always want to be on the boat. "We're taking the boat out this weekend. It's supposed to be beautiful. Why don't you come? You never come. You're always working. You know how many people wish they would get invited to come on the boat? And you turn it down."

Then you finally go, and they show you the boat. And then they make fun of you for not knowing all the different names of the boat's parts, and they start rattling off lingo to you: "The planks by the stern. The hull is like a dragon. It's stitched by a loom. You got to check out the masts. It's got peasant propulsion. *Dette er et for vandelar strat Goths klangenden.*" And they boss you around. "Everybody over there should be over here, and everybody over here should be over there."

WEST INDIANS

The first big immigrant wave when I was young was from the Islands: Jamaicans in the early seventies; Haitians followed right after. They live side by side in Brooklyn, separated only by Rogers Avenue. The Jamaicans are more flamboyant and the Haitians are very low profile. The Jamaicans had a surge of popularity in the early seventies based on Jimmy Cliff's movie soundtrack *The Harder They Come.* Reggae started to blast everywhere and suddenly Flatbush

Avenue looked like Trenchtown. There were beef-patty and jerk-chicken places on every corner. There were only a few Jamaicans in my school and they all played soccer in Prospect Park. Soccer was so rare back then that people would stop and watch a bunch of dreadlocked Jamaicans playing soccer like it was a solar eclipse. It became cool for white girls to date Jamaicans before it was considered okay for them to date black Americans. You would hear people say, "I heard she's dating a black guy?" "Nah, he's Jamaican." It was different, even though nobody could explain why.

When I was in elementary school, the first Haitians showed up, and they were very poor. And the American black kids started making fun of this Haitian kid for his threadbare clothes and for being too dark-skinned. He pulled his belt off and challenged all of them to a fight. Belt fighting was a big thing back then, and the Haitians, for whom I gathered discipline at home did not consist of "time outs," were trained for belt fighting from their early years. They gained respect because they don't like to fight but, when provoked, they fight to the death. Cursing you in French the entire time.

The Guyanese and the Trinis are a whole nother party. And I do mean party. Trinidad alone invented the steel pan, soca, calypso, and the limbo. They live out in Jamaica and Kew Gardens and Richmond Hill, because a lot of them have Indian blood. Kew Gardens was just winding down and they were just getting ready to call it a night and then their cousins that got caught in traffic show up and it starts all over again. Even their sports go on for days. They all play cricket. Most high schools in New York City have cricket teams. In ten years there'll be a *Friday Night Lights* about cricket.

AFRICANS

You've got the used-to-be-white-ruled Africa, which is everything from South Africa to Zimbabwe to Kenya. Then you've got the wild-ass countries in the Congo and then the West Side, like Nigeria and Ghana. African cabdrivers from all of those places always listen to political radio. Why? Because they found out what happens when you don't listen. And so while you are trying to make it home after a long night, they will ask you things like, "What do you think of the G8 summit regarding post-crisis IMF funding?" And you say, "Um, is that a Nicolas Cage movie?"

I didn't meet any Africans until 1984, when my aunt was living in the Bryant Hotel on 54th and Broadway, which is now probably worth a hundred million but back then was an SRO. Except for her, the rest of the hotel was all African street peddlers. I still don't know why they got into the handbag, watch, and umbrella business, but I know that the Koreans were the wholesalers and the Africans were the vendors. And you still see the African-Asian connection on Canal Street and up Broadway in the 20s.

Africans have their own rivalries. They all think Nigerians are con artists and that Ethiopians are conceited. But mostly they all think that Americans, black and white, are spoiled.

CENTRAL AND SOUTH AMERICANS

The biggest new group in New York today is the Central Americans, all these tiny people walking around Corona and Jackson Heights, and also Sunnyside and Woodside. Now the Germans have left that area, they can fit twice as many Central Americans in those apartments. Every time I feel sorry that I wasn't 6'8" and 240 pounds like I was supposed to be, I think about how these small people feel having to deal with a bunch of multiracial, oversized ogres. No wonder they invented the human sacrifice. What could be more entertaining than getting all painted up and dragging some large bully up to the top of a temple, lopping his dumb head off, and watching it shoot down a waterslide? I'd be cheering, too.

Columbians were the first South Americans in Queens and they dominated. Jackson Heights was Colombian even back in the seventies, but they got really popular in the eighties. Do I even have to tell you why? Now the Colombian drug lords are a memory. They've lost half their power to Mexico. They used to be the man; now that they are older they can only play in the old-timers' game.

Argentina has been broke since the 1970s. They were in debt before being in debt was cool. They're the friend who always extended his credit, took vacations, had a nice car and nice clothes, all because he knew how to work the system. The last time they were big was 1978. They're Peter Frampton. On the flip side, Chile is the guy who's been saving his money. Everybody else in the family is in serious debt and Chile has to co-sign for all their apartments. He's afraid to leave the house. Every time he goes to a summit all the other South American countries are trying to hit on him for a loan.

Ecuador is endearingly crazy, like an actor in a Tim Burton movie. I'm basing this on the fact that if you go to Ecuadorian restaurants on Roosevelt Avenue they have giant dead guinea pigs—"*cuy*"—hanging up in the windows and eat them with glee.

* * *

A hundred years ago, immigrants who came over saw America as the land of opportunity, where they could make their fortune. It was like a non-rip-off Las Vegas resort. Not everybody hit it big, but enough people did. It was a good casino.

But at some point everyone stopped thinking of America as the land of plenty and started seeing it as evil. One year the teacher in school says, "Thursday is Thanksgiving. Kids, that was the day we let the Indians sit down to dinner with us. Very nice of us, wasn't it?" The next year, the

212

teacher is like, "Thanksgiving is a day of genocide. Let's all paint bloody-tear decals for the school windows."

Since the 1990s, white people have flooded into New York, but so have many new waves of immigrants, bringing something like 140 languages to the borough of Queens alone. Thank God for immigrants. They're the only ones who have any personality left. They still allow themselves emotions, judgments, and all those qualities that we are "evolving" past. I don't know what they're saying, but I can tell they're speaking honestly.

CONCLUSION

Future Fuchsia

I KNOW A LOT OF YOU PEOPLE ARE GOING TO READ THIS BOOK and say, "This guy's an asshole. He's not helping the racial divisions in this country. He's just trying to be funny and clever, and he's neither." Others will dismiss me as a typical older, but very handsome, white male. That's marginalizing (and objectifying), but if that's how you see me, so be it. I get it. So basically if you read this book and don't find it funny, it's not because it's not funny. It's because you're brainwashed to not laugh at ethnic humor. Remember this: It's never my fault. Either I'm funny and you love me, or I'm funny and you're socialized against me.

Here's what the political correctness doesn't see: the absurdity and beauty of New York City in all its crazy glory.

In Queens every block is a mix of South and Central American, Asian, Arabic, Eastern European, and African communities living in a begrudging coexistence. The apartments and houses are subdivided into seemingly impossible configurations. Families share bathrooms with single male day workers. Educated, city-raised bachelors share kitchens with illiterate mountain people. Most buildings are home to a combination of legal and illegal immigrants, often members of the same family. On some blocks, there's a cab in the driveway of 80 percent of the homes.

On Main Street, Flushing, there's the nail salon school, the Hong Kong Supermarket, the Korean superstore, a table tennis center, a mah-jongg center, and catering halls. Nearby streets contain Hindu temples, Korean churches, Chinese churches, Sikh temples, synagogues, and mosques. Even early in the morning there are old people playing Chinese chess on the benches in the small parks, and people on bikes delivering recently slaughtered livestock. There are blocks on Northern Boulevard where transvestites blast reggaeton out their windows while the booming gay population walks up to the string of same-sex bars that can be found on the stretch of Roosevelt Avenue by 74th known as "Vaseline Alley." In the Colombian section, the dress code in summer for the women is Private Beach.

Underneath the 7 train runs Roosevelt Avenue, where the streets are filled with Ecuadorians, Guatemalans, Peruvians, and Mexicans, Mexicans, Mexicans. You can see clothing stalls with Mandarin signs, jewelry stores with Hindi and Punjabi writing, multinational uniform stores where you can purchase restaurant and hospital employee attire, *cambiamos cheques*, even a McDonald's where everything is in Spanish.

At the city agencies, there are babies crying, people yelling into cell phones, burned-out employees and petitioners trying to get through the bureaucratic nightmare that is life in the slow lane.

At Willets Point, where you find the New York Mets' Citi Field, there are auto-body salvage shops and train yards adjoining Flushing Meadows Park, where teenagers drink and hook up, homeless people sleep on benches, families picnic, and raccoons and squirrels and rats run wild. It's beautiful, even if it's hard to find something that hasn't been touched or slept on or pissed on or jerked off on by ten different people.

This city is better than any homogenized blocks where everyone is friendly as long as you don't say anything "insensitive," as if people bumping up against each other's cultures is automatically part of a "bigger problem," one that calls for a national dialogue and collective soul-searching.

To me, Queens looks like the mosaic of the future. Hybrid races may ultimately be what stops racial division. In a thousand years, we'll have a planet full of Croatian-Eskimo, Indo-Latvian, Jewish-Siberian kids—a master future race of unstoppable cyborgs. Dominicanadians will be loud and polite at the same time. Puerto-Russians already exist in Brighton Beach. They're highly bejeweled street-smart girls who talk fast and yet project an air of hopelessness.

The first interracial date was Sammy Davis Jr. and Kim Novak, and that didn't last because the Mafia said they were going to cut his other eye out. Interracial dating started, as I said, with Jamaican men and white women in the seventies. Then you had the Puerto Ricans and Irish starting to date because Puerto Rican women are bossy (forbidden sexist word) and Irish guys want to date someone who's exotic and yet will still tell them what to do all the time. It's a cultural thing. Irish guys are generally very quiet in the home and the women do most of the talking, and Puerto Rican women are comfortable with that dynamic.

There are still arranged marriages in India and Pakistan, but it's hard to judge that when you look at the average American online dating profile: *Must be women or in general vicinity...I'm not picky but prefer close to the N train...If I come over to your house, where would I leave my dog?...My hobbies include throwing coasters at Applebee's waitresses and standing outside the movie theater yelling the endings of kid movies...* Suddenly, "You're marrying the neighbors' son Ravi next Tuesday. Be there." Doesn't sound so bad.

But I'd like to suggest that given all the crazy metrics people use to figure out who they should go out with—astrology, for example—dating by race may be more helpful. Cultural differences aren't set in stone, but they have more to do with your personality than the alignment of the stars. For example, if you're having a hard time with fertility, you should date Latinos. You'll have grandkids by the time you're thirty. If you're into the most sexual but yet nonsexual sex of your life, you should go for someone Scandinavian.

Asian guys complain that Asian girls are always dating white guys. It's definitely true in Tribeca, where I live: Most of the families I see are made up of Jewish guys, Asian women in full tiger-mom mode, and their Caucasian-Asian babies. It's because Asian women are the opposite of Jewish women. The men finally get a word in edgewise. As I said, the Jews love culture, only now are they being joined by Asians. That's probably where the Jewish guys and Asian girls meet.

I have always liked Jewish girls myself, because of our differences. They were attracted to my who-cares, spontaneous, let's-change-the-plan attitude (manic depression), and I was attracted to their always looking for something fun and interesting to do (museums). They like to complain, but it's set against the backdrop of going out, which makes it better than complaining at home.

The Puerto Ricans have always felt free to date anyone—black, white, or anybody they liked. They've always had *carte blanco* when it comes to such matters, and thank God, because they play such a numbers game that they need an ever-expanding playing field. The guys are famous for inquiring as to your status. They actually used to be surprised if you came back from a date and said you didn't get laid.

"No?"

"No, she said she wasn't into it."

"She wasn't?" Then they'd think about it for a while. "But not even like...nothing?"

"No"

"Not like a handjob even?"

"No. I would've remembered a handjob."

Then they'd shake their head and mutter to themselves, "She looked like she was into it," and then just shrug and try to shake it off as a bad memory.

The heart wants what it wants. Some girls just like Irish guys. There's no accounting for it. Psychiatrists always say girls are searching for their father and boys are searching for their mother. That sounds pretty disgusting, but they don't mean sexually. They mean the personality. So you might think you're attracted to The Rock because he's a charming half-Samoan, half-Black, Nova Scotian (yes, it's disturbing to me, too) movie star, but it's really because, like your dad, he's a distanced introvert who withholds his love from you.

In theory, every woman wants a guy who loves his mother. In practice, no. You want a guy with a damaging mother so you can control him. You can give him the love he didn't get from his mother one day, which he loves, and then the next day you can treat him badly, which he loves even more, because then you remind him of his mean mother. It's like how football coaches never want the kids with the great home lives. A good football coach is a substitute dad for the kid. If a kid has a good father, the coach can't manipulate and control him. When I took martial arts, the teacher would give some insane order and the kids with self-worth would be like, "No fucking way." The kids who were insecure and unhappy grabbed their partner's balls without hesitation.

We can learn about dating confidence from black guys. True story: I once saw a black guy handcuffed against a police car and when a girl walked by, he said, before being driven away, "What's up, sweetheart?"

From the Puerto Ricans, we can learn about planning ahead. I remember one time when a Puerto Rican guy that I worked with at the liquor store in my neighborhood was hitting on a pregnant girl. "She's pregnant!" I exclaimed in outrage. "Yeah, but she's gonna have that baby and she'll be fine again," he explained. I had never heard of the lay-away plan for dating. From Italians you learn, "You can get more with a kind word and car, than you can from a kind word."

Dating sites say mixed-race people are the most coveted. We thought in the tech age we'd be post-racial. But even in Park Slope in the seventies you can see the foundation of social media sites in different ethnicities.

Black people are Twitter. That's no surprise. Black people have to assess everybody in under 140 characters: "That kid's fast, but you can tell by his face shape he's going to be a fat teenager."

Well, back then, our Twitter was the people sitting on the stoop chiming in on whatever passed by. The trolls in our neighborhood were these two old ladies, roommates, who used to walk up our block and scream at each other and the world. When they walked out of their house, shopping cart in tow, we'd all be waiting to see how long it took for the screeching to start. Sometimes they'd make it a whole block before they started yelling. Sometimes they'd make it half a block. But sure enough, within minutes, one would erupt with something along the lines of, "You son-of-a-bitch motherfucker!" And off they'd go.

Puerto Ricans were always talking, slipping in and out of Spanish. The way they talk, they bring you in. I don't know if it's the vowels or what, but it's sensuous and inviting. Taunting sexually. They include you in the conversation, saying things like, "What am I going to do?" And then, "No, really?" There are no rhetorical questions in Spanish.

They reiterate. "So you doin' good though, no? Well, I lost my job. But other than that, things are pretty good. You workin'?"

So Puerto Ricans were Facebook. They'd give you their personal life and would update you on who they ran into, what they did last night, how their girlfriend broke up with them and their relationship status is single ... Give you every blow-by-blow of their entire life. Show you their photos. "She's fine, right? No, that's her sister ... That's her on the right. What's wrong with you? You think I would say *she's* fine?"

The Italians were Instagram, because they'd *have* to give you a visual. "I was like *this*," they'd say. And then they'd run their hand over their face to show you how their face was stoic. And the Italians, with their "Go down there and tell them you're Frank's grandson," were also LinkedIn.

The Jews were Yelp. They like to review: "You ever go to the pizza parlor on 14th and Sixth? They give you a slice but it tastes like cardboard."

The Irish at the bar were Reddit. The bartender would start the thread: "See how the mayor only plowed the Upper East Side?" That would launch a thread about municipality that by the time they got to the end of the bar would be a guy yelling about the Paris peace talks.

* * *

Everyone moves out to the suburbs with this idea of what life should be like. It takes two generations on Long Island for a group of people to say, "Okay, our mistake. This isn't actually what we wanted." Long Island at this point knows its shit. New Jersey still thinks, "Hey, this could still work."

The suburbs as a concept were a mistake. We should have just had the country and the city and that was it. But the beauty of America is that we always believe we can have the best of both worlds. You can have the city and the country in one pseudo-city, pseudo-country place. You can be African and American. You can be a Jew for Jesus. The whole point of America is trying to have our cake and eat it, too. The Statue of Liberty should be holding a big piece of seven-layer chocolate.

Everyone asks, "Why would you write a book about race? Why even bring it up?" The point is I *want* to talk about it, and it shouldn't be a national crisis if I do. People keep saying we need to have a conversation about race, but this is the quietest conversation I've ever been in. Hello? Is anyone here? Anyone?

Acknowledgments

Ben Greenberg and Maddie Caldwell. Ben unruffled. Maddie fiery, passionate. If you told anybody who knows me that I would be sitting down in an office from 9 to 5, going through the editing and writing process and not jumping out of my skin, they wouldn't believe it. I don't believe it even now. But I miss Ben's bemused tranquillity when he says, "Wait, go back for a second," when he reads a line that sounds off for some reason, and Maddie sighing in frustration and recoiling and slumping down distraught over a badly phrased thought. The way you two believe in the importance of every sentence is incredible. You have made me admire and love editors.

Ada Calhoun. People say, "Without you, this book wouldn't have happened." You're a beautiful Scandinavian Fitzcarraldo who brought the ship over the mountain.

Acknowledgments

To my manager, Brian, thanks for having the confidence in and love for me and my work.

My agent Mike, for wanting to work with me for the pure love of the art. I won't tell anyone, don't worry.

To Gil and Robert and Larry at Grubman Indursky Shire. You guys do so much work to make this happen, and I won't tell the rich clients how much you let me slide on hours.

To Lia and RZO, thanks. I love you and you know I'll never be able to thank you even though I'm saying it.

To Jen, I love you. You amaze me constantly.

Chris Rock, we helped teach each other when we were confused beginners. And now you inspire every comedian, including me, every time you step onstage.

"Big Jer" Seinfeld. You are a friend beyond comprehension. You shaped modern stand-up comedy and you still have the humility to do the dirty work because you know it's an unsolvable riddle.

To the Comedy Cellar, my second home.

To Adam Sandler, you have been loyal to all your friends since the paper moon.

To Lorne Michaels, boss of all bosses.

To all the comics, I love us. Please don't ever become preachy or inflexible. If we don't see the contradictory nature of all sides of all issues (including our own), then who will?

To all my relatives—we shaped each other from all those early years. I don't know if everybody has the percentage of smart, broke people that we have in our family, but it's unbelievable. We are like the parallel-universe Kardashians.

To my brother and sister. We were the house that everyone came over to. All my friends loved you, not just because you played cards and basketball with them, but because you were great kids. And you have great kids. My nephews and nieces. What a world you live in. I admire the way you handle yourselves.

To my father. You would be so proud that I finally wrote a book. All that drinking together back when, and the love you showed no matter what I did. You were a great man. Love you, Pop.

To my Mom, the girl who couldn't lie. You have no charm, let's face it. Nobody that's ever met you can imagine you being fake for one second. You say it like you see it and you accept the consequences. Your brutal honesty is real love and everybody lucky enough to have known you knows that. I love you, Ma.

To everybody that grew up in Park Slope and Coney Island in the seventies. Especially Gwenn. It's hard to describe what it was like back then. Fucked up, but magic. I'm glad I was there.